THE TUNNELS OF TARCOOLA

THE TUNNELS OF TARCOOLA

JENNIFER WALSH

ALLEN&UNWIN

SYDNEY · MELBOURNE · AUCKLAND · LONDON

First published in 2012

Copyright © Jennifer Walsh 2012

Allen & Unwin
83 Alexander Street
Crows Nest NSW 2065
Australia
Phone: (61 2) 8425 0100
Fax: (61 2) 9906 2218
Email: info@allenandunwin.com
Web: www.allenandunwin.com

A Cataloguing-in-Publication entry is available from the
National Library of Australia
www.trove.nla.gov.au

ISBN 978 1 74237 675 2

Cover and text design by Ruth Grüner
Cover photos by house Quavondo (house), Terryfic3D, mangojuicy,
Anna Godfrey, Kasper Rasmussen, thinair28 / iStockphoto
Set in 11.1 pt Minion Regular by Ruth Grüner
Printed in Australia in November 2011 at McPherson's Printing Group,
76 Nelson St, Maryborough, Victoria 3465, Australia.
www.mcphersonsprinting.com.au

1 3 5 7 9 10 8 6 4 2

JENNIFER WALSH grew up in a country town, the youngest of three girls. When she and her sisters weren't jumping off haystacks, they were reading. Their father also read aloud to them, starting with *Great Expectations* and B*lack Beauty* and proceeding to stories he made up himself. Jennifer became a teacher, later worked in the theatre for some years, then 'accidentally' became a writer of computer user guides, a job that took her around the world.

Jennifer lives in Balmain in Sydney's inner west with her husband, actor Bruce Spence, and a tortoiseshell cat. *The Tunnels of Tarcoola* was inspired by the abandoned coalmines that really do exist under much of Balmain.

1

'OUCH!' Martin O'Brien threw his arms over his head to ward off a shower of stones as his sister slithered down the low cliff-face after him.

'Stop, Kitty. Wait!' But before he could get out of the way she had cannoned into him and they had landed in an untidy pile on the narrow beach.

'Where've you been?' said Andrea, scrambling over the rocks to join them. 'You said you'd come straight after school.' There was sand in the damp hair, dyed red and black, that dangled over her forehead.

'We got sprung. Martin had to do his homework before we could go out.' Kitty had pulled her shoes and socks off and was splashing about in the shallows.

'Come round here!' called David. 'We've found something really cool.'

'You mean *I've* found something really cool.' Andrea led the way around the point. Above them the cries of small children playing in the park floated on the warm spring air. People would be walking their dogs, mothers gossiping, the usual drunks slumbering peacefully in the grass. But down here at the base of the cliffs it was a different world, far from the city, far from the school on the next headland, far from the terrace houses towering over the bay.

The park had been the centre of their lives since they were toddlers being pushed on the swings. They had played their first ball games there, tippety-run cricket on long summer evenings, soccer when the days turned cool. They had had birthday parties and family picnics there, fathers lugging the heavy portable barbecues. Now they were free to go to the park on their own, but Kitty and Martin's cautious parents had said they weren't to go down to the water. Martin wished he had parents like David's, who treated him as an adult and let him do whatever he liked. Andrea could do whatever she liked too, because her mother didn't seem to notice; and Andrea liked to do lots of things, especially if they were dangerous.

'Everything's really weird today,' she called back. 'The tide's just gone way out, the way it does when a tsunami's about to hit, you know? So suddenly there was a whole new beach and then pow! I saw it!'

Now Kitty and Martin saw it too. The retreating tide had uncovered hard-packed sand and dark rocks of all sizes, including some they'd never seen before.

'Hey, these are the Stepping Stones!' cried Kitty, her round face pink with exertion as she tried to keep up with the others on her short legs. 'Look, they're sitting on the sand. And this has to be the Doughnut!'

The Doughnut was the first of a line of rocks that stretched across the water – stepping stones only for the brave, because you had to jump a long way from rock to rock. Now, with the tide way out, you could see that the hole in the centre of the Doughnut was very deep.

'It's a giant toilet!' Kitty giggled, climbing onto it. 'Only all the water's gone!' She shoved her head into the hole and shouted, 'Hellooooo!'

Her long plait dangled over her eyes as she straightened up. 'No echo?'

'It's better than that,' said Andrea. 'There's a cave.'

Martin looked around. 'Where?'

'Look,' said David. 'It's . . .'

'I'm showing them.' Andrea pushed him aside. 'It's my cave!' She climbed onto the Doughnut and lowered herself into the hole. Her head disappeared, and a moment later they heard her voice, faint and slightly hollow. 'Come on!'

'Oh, wow!' Kitty dropped her shoes and socks and scrambled into the hole. Martin followed, and they got into an awkward tangle before they managed to work out how to squeeze through the narrowest section.

At the bottom, the shaft curved towards the cliff-face. Martin wriggled awkwardly, feet-first, into a cavern big enough to stand up in. Most of it was filled with water, now just ankle-deep, and there were constant drips from above. An eerie green light came through the hole in the Doughnut, and from other cracks and fissures in the cave walls.

'Got your Gadget, David?' muttered Martin. David whipped it out of his pocket. His father had brought the Gadget back from Japan, and it had everything: screwdrivers, scissors, a fan with detachable blades and even a little torch, all folded up like a pocket knife.

Now David was playing the torch beam around the cavern. Andrea pointed. 'Look, this gets better and better. A tunnel!'

Sure enough, a fissure at the back of the cave opened into a narrow tunnel, winding downwards and to the left. David peered into it.

'Great!' he said. 'Let's get ropes and proper torches. Maybe if we come back on Saturday . . .'

'Oh, come on, David!' implored Andrea. 'Let's explore it now. Hey, it probably doesn't go very far.'

'I really don't think we should,' said David firmly. 'I think the tide's on the turn, and it's a bit late. What do you think, Marty?'

'Yeah, what do you think, Marty?' Andrea had that dangerous look in her eye. 'Are you scared too?'

'Course not.' Martin felt his cheeks burning. To tell the truth, if he was scared of anything these days it was Andrea. When they were younger everyone used to say she was his girlfriend. For all he knew she still was – it was just that he couldn't remember ever deciding that, or having a conversation with her about it. He looked apologetically at David. 'How about we just go a little way in?'

David shrugged. 'Okay, okay. Just having my say.' The others pressed close behind him as they entered the tunnel. The light from David's torch was weak, but in his flapping white shirt he was easy to see at the head of the little procession.

Kitty brought up the rear, clinging to the back of Martin's T-shirt. He could hear her muttering crossly, 'And what about you, Kitty? What do *you* think we should do? Oh, what do *I* think? You're asking *me*?'

The tunnel dipped, then wound upwards, and the sandy floor gave way to rough rock. At one point David jumped, and Andrea gave a little scream.

'Sorry,' said David. 'Something brushed my cheek.'

'Orcs!' breathed Martin. 'Or maybe – could it be – the Balrog?'

'Shut up, Marty!' David shone the torch beam on the roof. Here and there bunches of tree roots had penetrated the rock.

'I reckon we're right under the park,' said Martin.

'No way.' Kitty was quite definite. 'We've gone a lot further than that. We're somewhere near the Haunted House.'

They were still arguing the point when David stopped suddenly and they all piled into him. 'That does it,' he said, making a sweeping movement with his torch. 'We've got to go back and get proper equipment.'

Ahead of them was an intersection. A tall, narrow tunnel opened to the right. The tunnel they were in veered to the left, but it was low and round – they would have to stoop or crawl to get through it.

'I'm not going any further,' said David. 'We'll be lost in no time.'

'Okay, okay,' grumbled Andrea. 'But we're coming back

tomorrow, right? This is the best thing we've found since Fang!' Fang was the puppy they had found shivering on the beach the previous summer, now a large untidy dog who lived with Andrea's father in the country.

Since there was not enough room to pass each other in the narrow passage the Gadget was handed to Kitty, who led them back along the twisting tunnel.

'Do you think we could have gone wrong?' said David. 'It seems to be taking forever.'

'Well, we went a long way,' returned Martin. 'Look, it's sloping down now. We're nearly there.'

Suddenly Kitty stopped.

'Watch it!' hissed Andrea, almost falling over her.

'Ummm . . . Trouble.' Kitty's voice was shaking slightly. She shone the torch down the passageway ahead. They all saw the glint as its beam reflected on water.

2

KITTY edged down the slope and put a foot experimentally into the water to test the depth.

'How far do you think it is to the Doughnut?' she whispered.

'Dunno.' David pushed forward to look. 'Far enough.'

'How did it fill up so fast?' said Martin incredulously. 'The tide was so low.'

'Use your head, Marty,' snapped David. 'Didn't you see the gaps in the cave walls?'

'Okay, okay.' Martin felt his face burning. Sometimes he hated David.

'As soon as the water reaches the cracks, this tunnel starts filling up. It's lower than the cave.' David flashed the torch onto the murky water lapping at their feet. 'I should have thought of that.'

'Well,' said Andrea. 'Think about this: how are we going to get out?'

'I'll see how far it is,' said Martin, pulling off his T-shirt. 'I can swim fifty metres underwater.'

'No, Marty!' Kitty clutched his arm. 'It's all dark and twisty. What if you go the wrong way? There could be other passages we didn't notice.'

'She's right,' said Andrea. 'Or what if you get stuck, coming up through the Doughnut?'

'I suppose you're right,' said Martin, relieved that he didn't have to enter that dark water. 'So I guess we just wait for the tide to go out?'

'Sure,' said David. 'It'll be low again in about twelve hours.'

'Twelve hours!' shrieked Kitty. 'We can't wait that long! Mum and Dad'll kill us! Besides,' she added as an afterthought, 'I'm hungry.'

'We'll have to ring our parents,' said Martin. 'Can we use your phone, David?'

David looked briefly at his phone. 'No signal.'

'And before you ask,' said Andrea, 'I've got no credit.'

David was opening up his Gadget. 'The thing is,' he said, 'we might as well explore, right? We can use this blade to scratch arrows on the rock and mark our way.'

There was no response from the others.

'Come on!' said David. 'Do you want to just wait for the tide to come all the way in? It'll fill this tunnel, you know. Look around – everything's wet.'

'We'll drown!' gasped Kitty.

'Stop scaring her, David,' said Martin. 'The tunnel was dry further up, and you know it.'

David shrugged. 'Well, I'm going exploring, anyway. You lot can wait here if you like.' And he set off up the tunnel with his Gadget, leaving them in darkness.

'Da-a-a-vid!' They stumbled after him.

David led the way back along the tunnel, flashing the torch onto the walls. At least the rocky floor was dry, and there seemed to be enough fresh air.

Martin wondered if David knew things about tides that he didn't know. Probably – he was such a knowall. For example, might a very low tide be followed by one high enough to fill the whole of the tunnel system?

Soon they reached the intersection they had found before. David scratched an arrow, pointing back the way they had come, onto the sandy tunnel wall.

'Now what?' he said, looking at Andrea. Andrea looked at her feet.

David turned sideways and squeezed into the narrow passageway on the right. The others hesitated, watching as his torch beam flicked wildly about. Then there was darkness, and they crowded after him.

'Back! Back!' came David's muffled voice, and with much pushing and shoving they spilled out again.

'Fallen rocks,' he explained. 'Better try this way.' He ducked to enter the other passage, then flashed the torch back at them.

They crawled cautiously over dry rock. This tunnel was stuffy, with a sour smell. Martin yelped as his hand touched something sharp.

'Bones!' he said.

'We're going to die in here!' wailed Kitty.

'It's all right, Kitty,' said David. 'It's only a rat or something.'

'Rats!' shrieked Andrea.

'Pretty big one, too,' concluded Martin. Andrea moaned. Martin grinned in the darkness.

Meanwhile, the tunnel had gradually become wider and higher, and they were able to stand up again. They walked in single file, David occasionally flashing the torch around and above them. It was easy walking for a while, then they rounded one last bend and stopped.

'Another dead end,' sighed David.

'Wait a minute.' Martin edged forward. 'Give us the Gadget.' He shone the torch beam onto the wall in front of them. Then he scratched at the wall with the blade.

'What is it?' asked Andrea.

'This wall,' said Martin. 'It's kind of flat.'

'What do you mean?' Andrea ran the palm of her hand over the wall. 'Ouch! I've got a splinter!' she cried. 'This is wood.'

'Marty, you're a legend!' David took the Gadget and scratched around the edges of the wall, which was caked with dirt and grime.

'It's a door,' he said. 'But how do we get through? We've got to find the key.'

'Maybe it uses a secret lever,' suggested Martin, feeling around the sides.

'Do you think we should try some magic words?' contributed Kitty.

'Oh, come on,' said Andrea impatiently. 'Who says it's locked?'

She put her shoulder to the door and pushed. With rusty

hinges complaining, it swung stiffly open. They crowded through.

The door opened into a small, square chamber with grimy brick walls. On each of the four sides was an arch in the brickwork. In the one opposite them was another door. The other two arches had no doors, and led into darkness. To the left, a rusty iron ladder led upwards, towards faint lines of greenish light. There was a foul smell, like rotten eggs.

'Hey, you'd know what to do here, Marty,' said David. 'Now, let's see. If we go one way we'll have to answer a riddle; another way, fight a dragon or something; another way there'll be a dwarf who might give us information if we help him.'

'Or on the other hand he might hack us to death with his axe,' agreed Martin. 'So which way do you want to go?'

'Up,' said Andrea. 'Come on, this place stinks.' She clambered up the ladder. Martin started to follow, but David grabbed his arm.

'Wait,' he said. 'It might collapse if we all get on it.'

Andrea reached the top and scrabbled around, then she called down, 'I think I need some help.' Martin was up the ladder in a flash. It creaked alarmingly under the extra weight.

'There's a lid or something above me,' said Andrea. 'I guess it's a trapdoor. I can't lift it.'

'Let's try pushing it sideways,' suggested Martin. Clinging with one hand to the ladder, they both pushed hard at the obstruction.

A sliver of light appeared, and the others cheered. The gap

slowly widened as they kept pushing, and they heard a clatter as something fell over. When there was enough space Andrea climbed through, then the others scrambled up to join her. Martin saw that they had torn the hinges off the trapdoor, which had been covered by a pile of empty wooden crates.

They were in a large, dim underground room dotted with square brick columns. A couple of small barred windows on one side, just under the low ceiling, allowed in some light, but the rest of the space was in deep shadow. Here and there they could see gaps like narrow doorways in the rough stone walls. More wooden crates were littered about on the dirt floor, with a couple of broken chairs and a table with a missing leg.

'It's the Haunted House!' breathed Kitty. 'Didn't I tell you? We're in the cellar of the Haunted House.'

Everyone knew the Haunted House near the park, beside the deserted factory. It was only accessible by a narrow lane-way, and there was so much tangled wilderness of garden you could hardly make out the dark, brooding shape of the building.

'Oh, wow!' said Andrea. 'My sister saw the ghost once.'

'Wooooooooo!' Martin couldn't resist running around the columns and jumping out at her.

'Oh, very funny,' she sniffed.

'Rosa and I came here once,' said Kitty, ignoring this exchange. 'We looked in through the windows – those barred windows up there. I recognise them. And what's more, there's one with broken bars! I remember now! Come on.' Followed by the others, she scrambled through one of the narrow gaps into a similar space, a bit smaller and darker, festooned with cobwebs.

The cellar seemed to be a maze of odd-sized rooms, but after a bit of searching they found the window Kitty had seen. A couple of its bars were missing, and the others were twisted out of shape, leaving a gap big enough to climb through. It was a simple matter then to pile up enough old wooden chairs to climb on. Andrea and Kitty hopped up, and the boys shoved from behind.

'Wait a minute,' said David, pausing. 'I think we should push those crates back over the trapdoor, so no one else finds out about our tunnel.'

'Right,' agreed Martin. 'And we can come back tomorrow for a really good look.'

When they got outside, the two girls were sitting on an old wooden bench, talking.

'I don't care,' Andrea was saying. 'Lots of people have seen it. It kind of hovers at that window up there.' She pointed.

'You shouldn't tease Kitty,' said David. 'You know there aren't any ghosts.'

'She doesn't worry me,' Kitty assured him. 'Anyway, I'm more frightened of the snakes.'

'What snakes?'

'Cec says there are snakes in the garden. He's seen one. His back yard comes right up to the fence, you know, on the other side of the lane.'

'Cec is about a hundred, and he's got dementia,' scoffed Andrea. Still, she looked nervously around her. The darkening garden was an overgrown wilderness, with ivy creeping along the ground and up the walls of the house.

'That's crap!' protested Kitty. 'Cec knows all about this neighbourhood, doesn't he, Marty? Mum says his mind is clear as a bell.'

Martin was staring at Kitty's bare feet.

'Where are your shoes and socks, Kitty?'

'Oh.' There was a long silence. 'I think I left them next to the Doughnut. I'd better go back and get them.'

'Next to the Doughnut,' said David. 'On that beach? At low tide?'

'Um . . . Yes.'

Martin groaned.

3

'YOU talk to them, Paul.' Kitty and Martin's mother was using her very controlled voice. This was going to be bad.

'Do you children realise what you've put your poor mother through?' thundered Paul O'Brien. 'Do you realise that in five more minutes we would have called the police?'

'Kitty!' Although she always said 'You talk to them,' their mother could never stay out of it for long. 'Look at your school dress! And where are your shoes and socks?'

Kitty opened her mouth to tell the whole story, but Martin was faster.

'Mum, we're really sorry. Kitty lost her shoes in the park and we've been looking for them. We didn't want to come home without them.'

'Oh, Kitty, how could you be so careless! And what about your dress?'

Kitty wasn't very good at lying, and the distracting aroma of spag bol – her favourite – wafted from the kitchen.

'Oh . . . well, you know, I had to crawl under bushes and stuff. I'm really sorry, Mum.'

'You should never have been in the park so late. You said you were going to David's . . .'

And so it went on. The outcome was grounding for the rest of the week. Three days, not negotiable.

After dinner, Kitty and Martin meekly cleared away without having to be nagged,

'I think we got off okay,' Martin said quietly as he scrubbed the spaghetti pot.

Kitty nodded. 'It's a pity, though,' she said sadly. 'Now we'll have to wait until the weekend before we can explore those tunnels.'

They could hear a jumble of noise from the next room where their parents were watching the TV news – at least their father was, and he had plenty to say about it. Their mother was marking English assignments, chuckling now and then, occasionally giving a snort of exasperation and dashing her red pen through something.

Next morning Kitty got up very early and ironed her spare school dress. Then she hunted out a pair of Martin's old school shoes and polished them.

'Oh dear,' her mother said, her face softening at all this industry. 'I suppose you could have worn your trainers today.'

'No, Mum. We're going on an excursion. It's full school uniform.'

'Oh, did I sign the note? Have you got everything you need?'

'Sure thing.'

Kitty stuffed her lunch into her bag and flew out the door, leaving Martin to his Weet-Bix. Their schools were in the same general direction, but she liked to be early, whereas he thought it was cool to arrive right on the bell.

At school, Mr Mac gave out instructions and handouts in the first session, then the whole of Year Six, both classes, set out on foot, clutching their clipboards. Local history was the subject, and where better to find some, said Mr Mac, than by interviewing the occupants of the Sunset Home for the Aged?

The Sunset Home was a lovely old house with stained-glass windows in a quiet street. There must have been a big garden once, but now it just had extra buildings and parking areas. A fat girl in a pink uniform and a couple of men in white overalls hovered by a side entrance, smoking and gossiping.

Once inside, Kitty and her classmates were rounded up in a wide entrance hall and given a talking-to by the Matron. *Remember, children, some of these people are quite frail and easily upset. You must all be very quiet.*

'Betcha I get a deaf one. Will I still have to be quiet then?' Rosa whispered in Kitty's ear, and they both giggled.

'Katherine O'Brien?'

'Here, Miss.'

'Miss Gordon, Ward E. It's a single room, up the stairs, first on the left. Call the nurse if you have trouble with her.'

What sort of trouble? wondered Kitty as she climbed the stairs.

Miss Gordon was sitting by her bed facing the window, where you could just see the tops of the trees in the park. She had a bony back and clouds of white hair.

Kitty cleared her throat. There was no response. She

coughed. Miss Gordon kept gazing out at the treetops. Kitty reached forward tentatively and touched her shoulder.

The old lady turned. Her face was a maze of wrinkles, her blue eyes vacant.

'Miss Gordon? My name's Kitty. I have to interview you – for my school, you know. I have to ask you some questions.'

The blue eyes slowly, dreamily, came to rest on Kitty's face.

'Eh?'

Kitty started again. 'Do you mind if I ask you some questions about your life?'

'Questions? Yes, dear.'

'Um . . . Okay.' Kitty hoped that meant she didn't mind. 'So . . . um . . . Before you were in the Home, where did you live?'

'Where did I live? Didn't they tell you, dear?' Miss Gordon drew herself up proudly. 'Tarcoola. I was the mistress of Tarcoola.'

'Oh. Really? Tarcoola?' Kitty wrote it down. 'Is that near here?'

'Near here?' The old lady looked around vaguely. 'It's by the water. You could watch the sailing boats go by. Ask anyone, dear. Everyone knows Tarcoola. They should have told you.'

She seemed to shrink into herself, frowning, and turned away from Kitty, lost in some vision of the past.

'It sounds lovely,' said Kitty. 'Tarcoola!'

'Oh, yes.' The old lady turned back. 'The parties we had! The ladies in their frocks. All the big cars, coming up the driveway.'

This sounded promising. Kitty wrote it down.

'Is that where you were born?' she asked next.

'I should think not, dear. I was born in Christina Street. There on the corner of Forrester's Lane. Do you know it?'

'Oh, yes, I do! My friend lives in that street. I go there all the time.'

'It was a good street.' Miss Gordon smiled. 'Our house had two bedrooms, you know, and a scullery. And Mother had her roses.'

'What school did you go to?'

'Well, we all went to the nuns. I had five brothers and three sisters, and where Mother got the money for the uniforms I don't know, after they closed the Pit. Everything had to be spick and span in those days. Do you go to the nuns, dear?' She seemed to focus for the first time on Kitty, with her neatly plaited hair and polished shoes.

'Oh no. I go to the public school, you know, over the road from the . . . from the nuns.'

There was a slightly frosty silence, and Kitty looked at the notes she had scribbled.

'Excuse me, what was the Pit?'

'Hmmm?'

'You said, "after they closed the Pit."'

'Oh, it was a shame, yes, with all the miners out of work. Father had to go back to the wharves and there wasn't much there either, once the Depression started. It was a terrible time, with all the younger ones still at home.'

'So the Pit was a mine?'

'Yes, dear, the coal mine. But you don't want to know about that. It's all gone now. Father always said it was a good thing none of the boys would be going down the Pit. Did I tell you I had five brothers?'

'Yes. Does that mean there were nine children in your family?'

'Nine? Nine. Yes. I suppose that's right. Five boys and four girls. And a couple more little ones that Mother lost.'

'Oh. How did she lose them?' Kitty supposed that with more than nine children trailing behind, you might easily lose one or two.

'Well, I think it was the diphtheria, but one died of the Spanish Flu just before I was born. Poor Mother – she always took it so hard. I was one of the youngest, and Mother hoped I would stay at home and help her. But I had to go into service like my sisters.'

Kitty understood now about the lost babies. Her mother liked wandering through old churchyards on holidays, and they had seen many family graves, sad little lists of babies and young children buried with nearly every 'wife of the above'. She was puzzled, however, as to what 'service' meant. The Army, or the Navy?

'So what happened when you were in the service?'

'Work! You young people today . . . Up before dawn, washing and scrubbing. We blacked the stove every day, first thing, before it was lit. I hate to think how much hot water I carried up those stairs. It was three years before I was allowed to touch the silver. Lovely silver they had – not as good as Tarcoola, though. Mr Wolf liked to have the best, always the best. He brought such beautiful things with him from Europe.'

Kitty was floundering. She searched for clues.

'Um . . . did you wear a uniform, in the . . . in service?'

'Oh yes. They were old-fashioned there, of course – the black dress, everything starched – even the little white cap. I wasn't any bigger than you are when I started, dear. When I put the apron on you could hardly see me at all! Like a walking tent!'

They both laughed. Miss Gordon sighed.

'I hope you don't have to go into service, dear.'

'Oh! I don't think so. I'm going to be a vet.'

Miss Gordon clearly wasn't listening. Her gaze strayed back to the trees.

'I was good to the girls at Tarcoola. Mr Wolf never understood that. I didn't take any nonsense, though.'

Kitty was wondering if she would ever be able to make sense of her notes.

'So . . .' she ventured, 'was Mr Wolf your boss?'

'I beg your pardon!' Miss Gordon drew herself up. 'Mr Wolf was my husband. Didn't I tell you I was mistress of the house?'

Kitty became aware of someone behind her. It was Rosa, jiggling with impatience.

'Come on, Kitty! Everyone's downstairs waiting.'

'In a minute.'

Kitty turned back to the old lady. 'I'm sorry,' she said. 'I have to go now.' She held out her hand.

Miss Gordon – or was it Mrs Wolf? – took Kitty's hand and held it against her cheek. Despite the wrinkles, her skin was soft and cool.

'Goodbye, then, dear. What did you say your name was?'

'Kitty.'

'What a lovely old-fashioned name. It's been so nice having a chat.'

Kitty quickly stacked her notes and glanced at the printed question sheet on top.

'Oh, I'm sorry,' she said. 'I forgot to ask you about your birthday.'

Miss Gordon drew back suddenly. 'Don't you ask about that!' Her voice was a harsh whisper.

'Oh. Okay.'

'They all kept asking me,' mumbled the old lady. 'But I wouldn't tell them. It's yours, he said.'

'It's okay,' said Kitty. 'I won't ask. I'm sorry.'

She took Miss Gordon's hand. After a moment the blue eyes focused on her.

'You will come and see me soon, won't you?' said the old lady, as if nothing had happened.

'Yes, if I can.'

Rosa was waiting outside. 'I think I might have got the wrong person!' whispered Kitty. 'But she was a bit muddled, so I can't be sure.'

They passed a plump nurse who was heading into the ward.

'Wait a minute,' Kitty muttered. She ran after the nurse. 'Excuse me! That lady in there, what's her name?'

'That's Clarissa. Miss Clarissa Gordon.'

'Oh, it was the right one. She said she was married to someone called Mr Wolf.' Kitty couldn't help giggling a little.

'She thinks she was, poor thing.' The nurse leaned a little closer. 'Bigamy!' she breathed.

'Oh!' What was bigamy, Kitty wondered. 'Well, anyway, would I be allowed to visit her again?'

'Yes, of course. It does them good to have visitors. She doesn't see anyone except the priest from one year to the next.'

'Thanks.' Kitty ran back to Rosa.

'What's bigamy?' she asked as they hurried down the stairs.

'Oh, it's . . . um . . . I'm sure I've heard of it . . .'

'It's a great story,' continued Kitty. 'She used to be a servant, I think, but she ended up really posh. She says she was mistress of Tarcoola.'

'No kidding!' gasped Rosa. 'Tarcoola?'

'Yes, do you know where that is?'

'Course I do. Didn't you see the name above the door?'

Kitty looked blank.

'When we went in that time?' persisted Rosa. 'The name's carved above the front door.'

She paused for effect. 'The Haunted House!'

4

ON the way back to school, Kitty was the centre of attention. It seemed that many of the other inmates of the Sunset Home had been unwilling to talk about themselves, but only too eager to talk about Miss Gordon.

'What's the deal with her?' asked Anna. 'My old lady kept saying things like "Airs and graces", and calling her Lady Muck. But then the old lady next to her leaned over and said there was such a thing as charity, and kept calling your Miss Gordon "Poor thing". What did she do?'

'I don't know,' said Kitty. 'But what does bigamy mean?'

'Hear that?' Scott elbowed Jason, obviously delighted to find something Kitty did not know. 'She hasn't heard of bigamy!' Jason grinned uneasily.

'It's when a person gets married twice,' contributed Caitlin, looking up from the book she was reading as she walked along, steered by Anna.

'Only twice—?' started Rosa.

'Yeah, yeah, we know your auntie's been married seven-teen million times,' Scott interrupted. 'But she was divorced in between, wasn't she? Bigamy's when you're married to two people at the same time, and it's breaking the law.'

'So Miss Gordon did that?' said Rosa. 'Why don't they just get over it?'

'Anyway,' said Kitty. 'I don't think she did it. I'm guessing it was kind of done to her. That's why she's still Miss Gordon, and not Mrs Wolf, or whatever the name is. But the best part is, she lived in the Haunted House!'

'Hey, maybe she's the ghost?' put in Jason.

'You can't have a ghost who's still alive,' scoffed Rosa. 'But maybe she murdered the other wife when she found out? What do you reckon?'

'Ooooooooohhhh!' Several boys saw this as a chance to practise their ghost impersonations.

'I'm not going back to that place, that's for sure,' shuddered Karen. 'Those people smell.'

'Maybe she murdered her husband, and he's the ghost?' mused Rosa.

'She wouldn't tell me when her birthday was,' Kitty said. 'She was really funny about it – as if it was some big secret.'

'Sounds like my auntie,' said Rosa. 'If you ask how old she is, she always says twenty-one. How dumb is that?'

After school, Rosa said, 'Do you want to come to my house? Or are you meeting Andrea?'

'Sorry,' said Kitty. 'I'm grounded.'

She told Rosa about losing her shoes at the foot of the cliffs, but no more. It wasn't so much because of the boys, though they would not be pleased if Rosa turned up wanting to explore the tunnels with them. It was more to do with Andrea.

She didn't get on with any of Kitty's friends, so it could be awkward. Lately Kitty had found herself dividing her social life into Andrea days and Rosa days.

'Hey,' suggested Rosa, 'do you want to go past the Haunted House on the way home? It won't make you late, if we hurry. I'll show you the name above the door.'

They crossed the road that led to the park and walked up the narrow lane. There was barbed wire along the fence and over the gate, which was closed with a huge rusty padlock; but there were gaps big enough for them to climb through. The house was just visible through the trees.

They reached a path that meandered through the trees, then opened into a clear space. Cracked marble steps led up to a porch with elaborate pillars and the remnants of a beautiful tiled floor. Above, carved in stone and crumbling away in parts, you could read the name: 'Tarcoola'.

'You're right!' Kitty breathed. She gazed at the porch, seeing visions of ladies in long dresses, dripping with jewels, and men in hats and white silk scarves, sweeping up the drive in big old-fashioned cars. Maybe if she turned around she would see immaculate gardens, lawns rolling down towards the park, peacocks trailing their splendid tails.

'Wanna go inside?' Rosa whispered in her ear.

'I can't. I'll be toast if I don't get home.'

'I'll show you a shortcut,' offered Rosa, plunging off through the undergrowth again to the right. Kitty groaned, but followed her anyway.

There was just a crumbling stone wall between the house and the former factory next door. They crossed an expanse of concrete strewn with broken glass and rusted bits of machinery, some squat steel buildings with saw-toothed roofs, and a lot of weeds. Not so long ago, Kitty remembered, this factory had still been working, its low hum audible from her bedroom at night.

'This way.' Rosa was already up some steps at the far side of the factory. At the top there was a locked gate and a cyclone-wire fence with plenty of gaps. Kitty climbed through and looked back.

Between the gate and the first factory building there was a notice on a post, flapping in the breeze. It showed a faded plan of the site, divided up into tiny numbered rectangles. Kitty looked at the plan, trying to make sense of it. Something about it niggled at her brain.

'Thought you were in a hurry?' Rosa was pulling the broken bits of wire together to make the gap look less obvious.

Kitty said goodbye to Rosa at the corner, then ran most of the way home. When she was nearly there she spied Martin dawdling ahead of her.

'Guess what! Guess what!' she called. 'The Haunted House has got a name.'

'Yeah, Tarcoola. So?'

Kitty was deflated. 'You knew that?'

'Course. It's written right above the door.'

'I hate you, Martin.'

They walked in silence for a while.

'Anyway, that's not all,' Kitty resumed. 'I met someone who used to live there.'

'Yeah?' Martin slowed down. 'Who?'

'This old lady at the Sunset Home. I interviewed her. I've made notes . . .' Kitty groped in her bag.

'Did you ask her about the tunnels?'

'No, I didn't realise . . . But I'm going to see her again. She's a really sweet old lady, and she calls me "dear". She thinks Kitty's a lovely name.'

'Well, find out what she knows about those tunnels. But don't let on that we've been in there.'

'Oh, right. So I say, we don't know there are tunnels under your house, but why are they there and where do they go?'

'You'll think of something. Be subtle.'

As they arrived, their mother pulled up in the car, and Kitty helped her to carry in the groceries and put them away. Martin vanished into his room, pleading homework.

'How was your excursion?' asked their mother.

'Amazing! The place smelled a bit off, but my old lady was really nice.'

'Was she a local?'

'Sure was! She was born in Christina Street, near Andrea's place.'

'That's great. So I suppose she told you a lot about local history.'

'A bit, but we had to go. I want to talk to her some more.

I reckon I can do the best interview in the class. Can I go and see her again, Mum?'

'Seems like a good idea, love.'

'Only the trouble is . . .' Kitty put on her saddest face. 'I'm grounded.'

'Oh. Hmmm. Well, maybe we could make an exception, if it's schoolwork.'

Kitty threw her arms around her mother. 'Oh Mum, I knew you'd say that!' She got out the fresh bread and started making herself a sandwich.

'Mum, you know the Haunted House?'

'Yes, love.'

'Well, this lady I interviewed used to live there. She was the mistress of Tarcoola.'

'Really? She must have some stories to tell.'

'And before that she was in service. What does that mean?'

'Well, it means she was a servant. A housemaid. But I don't know how she'd go from that to being in charge of a big house like Tarcoola. Unless she means she was the housekeeper there.'

'I don't know. She talked about her husband as if he was the owner.' Kitty munched thoughtfully on her sandwich. 'Mum, why doesn't anyone live at Tarcoola? Is it because it's haunted?'

'Of course it's not haunted, Kitty. Kids just say that because it's empty, and a bit spooky. It's been empty for as long as I can remember, and it's so dilapidated now, I suppose it would cost too much to fix it up. Maybe Cec knows something about it.'

'Oh yes! Cec knows everything. Can I go and see him? It's

for school,' Kitty added hastily. 'So I can get more facts for my interview.'

'You can stay right here,' said her mother firmly. 'I'm sure you've got homework to do. Cec will probably come along the back lane soon, walking Sweetheart. I'll be keeping a lookout. I've been collecting up some old magazines for him.'

'Oh . . . okay.' Kitty gathered up her schoolbooks. 'Anyway, that house is haunted. I know lots of people who've seen the ghost.'

Kitty went into Martin's room.

'Go away,' he said, without turning around. 'I'm doing my Chinese homework.'

Kitty watched over his shoulder as he struggled with the mysterious characters.

'It must be funny learning to read if you're Chinese,' she observed.

'Funny? There are thousands of these things. I should've picked French.'

Kitty sorted out her notes, then took her project book to the dining table and opened the double doors. She sat drawing up her title page and listening. Bees buzzed lazily in the garden and her mother snip-snipped with the secateurs.

A faint wheezing sound could be heard, getting louder. A wattle-bird flew up from the banksia tree with a raucous cry of protest.

'I think that's them,' said her mother. Kitty ran down the path and opened the back gate.

'Hello, Cec!' she called.

Sweetheart wheezed louder at the sight of Kitty and waddled towards her, dragging Cec on the other end of the leash. It was hard to guess what breed she was supposed to be when all you could see was a balloon from which four little legs stuck out. She looked like the drowned dog Kitty and Martin had once seen floating in the harbour. Cec, by contrast, was wiry and spry. He wore a straw hat, a threadbare white shirt and trousers held up by a piece of rope. He raised his hat at the sight of Kitty.

'Hello, little lady!' He suffered himself to be dragged through the gate as Sweetheart snuffled happily over Kitty's foot.

'Nice day, missus!' Cec raised his hat to Kitty's mother too.

'Hold on a minute, Cec,' she said. 'I've got something for you.' She disappeared inside the house.

'Cec,' said Kitty casually, 'did you know the people who lived in the Haunted House?'

'Well, now. That place's been empty for as long as I can remember.'

'Are you sure?' Kitty tried to hide her disappointment.

'Yep. We've been in our house since just after the war, and there's never been anyone in that old place, to my knowledge. Unsafe, I'd say. Saw a snake in the garden once.'

'Yes, I know. Have you ever seen the ghost?'

'There's no ghost there.' He chuckled and reached down stiffly to pat the dog. 'Sweetheart'd know if there was ghosts.'

'Really?'

'Course. Dogs can sense ghosts, all right. But she's always trying to get in there. There's wild cats in that yard, and she's mad keen to chase them.'

The thought of Sweetheart attempting to chase anything made Kitty giggle. Fortunately her mother reappeared at that moment with an armful of magazines.

'Here you are, Cec. There's this month's *Gardening Australia* and a few copies of *Better Homes and Gardens*. And how's Win? Keeping well?'

'Her leg's bad, missus, but she's good in herself, like. Well, thanks for these. I'd better be off. Sweetheart wants her tea. Got some nice rump for her tonight.'

'That dog eats too much! Put her on a diet, Cec.'

'Well, she's not getting any sweets!' And Cec allowed Sweetheart to drag him away down the lane as if she could already smell home and supper. Kitty stood at the gate, watching them. Just before they turned the corner a thought struck Cec.

'I did hear the chap committed suicide,' he called.

'What?'

'In that house. During the war?'

'Suicide? Cec! Was his name Mr Wolf?'

But Cec had gone. Sweetheart, on the home stretch and almost within scent of her rump steak, was unstoppable.

5

ANDREA squatted at the clifftop, looking down at some boys climbing over the Stepping Stones. When the rocks hid them from view Andrea threw a stone into the Doughnut. She heard a soft splash.

She had waited for David, but just to tell him that the others couldn't come. As she'd expected, he had nodded and hurried off home.

'It's okay,' she thought. 'I know he doesn't like me.'

Her mind wandered back to the confrontation with her History teacher that afternoon.

'I can't see that there's any excuse for it,' Miss Tenniel had said. 'This is the third assignment in a row you haven't handed in. You were doing such good work at the beginning of the year. Is there something wrong at home?'

'No!' Andrea was jolted out of her sullen silence.

'Well, I'm going to give you one more chance, but this is the last time. I've spoken to your Year Adviser, and he feels that if there's no improvement we'll have to contact your parents.'

'You mean my mother.'

'No, Andrea. The school has your father's contact details too. We feel that both your parents are entitled to know what's going on. It's not just History, is it? You're falling down in all your subjects.'

Andrea's cheeks were burning.

'Please don't tell my father. It won't do any good.'

'We may have to, Andrea. As you know, we've written to your mother before, and there was no response. But if you complete this assignment and show some improvement in the rest of your work we'll wait and see. I'm giving you until Friday of next week.'

'I've lost the sheet.'

'I'm sure you have,' Miss Tenniel said resignedly, handing her another one. Andrea remembered, a little guiltily, how she had screwed hers up the day they were handed out and thrown it into the bin from the second-back row. Miss Tenniel was writing on the board at the time, and hadn't appeared to notice this feat, or the silent applause that accompanied it from the boys at the back.

Now, sitting back on her heels at the clifftop, Andrea dragged out the sheet and looked at it in despair. 'A Historical Biography,' she read. 'A family member, neighbour or friend. Include historical information. Up to one thousand words.' Who could she possibly do? Her mother? Not really old enough, and anyway, her mother's life was none of the school's business. Her grandparents? She didn't know anything about them, especially on her father's side.

Some people were lucky. David's funny-looking grand-father used to always pick him up from school. He had come

34

into the class once, when they were in Year Five, and talked about what the area was like in the old days, when he was growing up. 'Call me Moshe,' he had said to the children, sitting on the floor and waving his hands as he talked, his black eyes bright as a goblin's.

But there was no way she could go to David's house and ask his grandfather questions. She could just imagine what he would think of her.

Maybe Celeste could help? Andrea dismissed the thought almost as soon as it entered her brain. Her big sister was always on the verge of being suspended from school, and anyway she was hardly ever at home these days.

If only she could go and live with her father in the bush, make a fresh start. Last time he had come to visit, over a year ago now, she had suggested it – casually, not making a big deal of it.

'Not a bad idea, hon,' he had said. 'It's a bit rustic right now, but I'm gonna get some solar panels organised, fix things up a bit. I'll let you know, yeah?'

'Don't hold your breath, love,' her mother advised after he had gone.

She put the assignment sheet back into her schoolbag and left the park, dragging her feet. She was in no hurry to go home. Her mother would probably be at the pub. She'd be greeted by an empty house and a pile of dirty dishes left over from last night.

She crossed the road and stood at the end of the lane that

led to the Haunted House, thinking about the tunnels. How far did they go? she wondered. Maybe you could hide down there and never be found. Maybe there were other entrances inside the house, behind fireplaces or in secret rooms.

There was no one in sight. Andrea walked quickly up the lane and slipped through a gap in the fence. The house loomed large and forbidding in the late-afternoon light. She ran around to the side where they had found the unbarred cellar window and climbed in, dropping to the floor in a cloud of dust that made her sneeze.

It was gloomy in the cellar. The holes that led to other sections were smaller than she remembered, and swathed in cobwebs. Andrea tried to remember which one led to the place with the trapdoor. Gritting her teeth, she crawled through the nearest opening and jumped up, brushing imaginary spiders from her hair.

Andrea waited for a moment until her eyes got used to the darkness. This was definitely not the place. She was in a large windowless area. In one corner she could make out a wooden staircase leading steeply upwards, with a door at the top.

The banister was rickety, and the stairs creaked loudly as Andrea climbed up. She reached the top, heart pounding, and pushed tentatively at the door. It moved a little, then met resistance. Andrea pushed harder. There was a tearing sound, then the door swung stiffly open and she stepped through.

She was in a central hallway. Some distance along the hall she could see the front door, flanked by softly glowing panels of coloured glass. Dim light came through the doorway of the room across the passage. She could see double glass doors leading outside and through them the green haze of a garden. The room contained a pile of rubble and a gaping hole where presumably a fireplace had once been. There was a key in one of the glass doors. When she tried it, it turned easily in the lock. She considered slipping out and going home through the shadowy garden, but there was more to explore.

To the right of the front door, a magnificent staircase curved upwards. Andrea pressed herself against the wall, listening. There was a faint sighing, which might have been a ghost. But there are no ghosts, she reminded herself. Her heart was thumping.

She put a foot on the staircase and listened again. No change. Cautiously she climbed the stairs, all her senses on high alert.

At the top of the stairs there were several rooms. Andrea crept along, wincing when a floorboard creaked under her. Outside one room the sighing, moaning sound seemed to be louder. She peeped around the doorway, ready to run. The window in the room was cracked, and the sound came from several scraps of paper rustling on the broken linoleum. Andrea picked up one of the scraps. It was a yellowed old newspaper, brittle in her hand. She found a date: 1937.

Andrea relaxed a little. The house felt empty and deserted now, as if no one had been there since 1937. She peeped into the room opposite. It had a bay window, most of its panes broken, overlooking the tangled garden. She could see the big trees in the park, palms and Moreton Bay figs, and the water beyond. The remains of a huge old iron bed were still there, its knobs speckled with age. A broken dressing table stood beside it. Andrea opened the one remaining drawer, but there was nothing in it but scrunched-up newspaper.

As she was closing the drawer something caught her eye. She reached into the back of the drawer and pulled out a yellowed photograph, tattered at the edges as if something had been nibbling it.

Andrea squinted at the photograph, trying to make it out in the fading light. Somewhere in the house a door slammed.

She ran to the top of the stairs and peeped over the balustrade. Shadows were moving down below, and she thought she heard a voice. She edged back along the passage. At the end she found another narrow staircase. She half-ran, half slid down it, trying not to make a sound. At the foot, she could see the cellar door, still half open the way she had left it. She flitted across and groped her way down the lower staircase.

It was very dark at the bottom, and she could barely make out the openings that led to the other sections. Her sense of direction had deserted her, and she couldn't remember which one led to the broken window and her escape. She found an opening and climbed through. It wasn't right. She was halfway back through the opening when she heard a creak.

Andrea froze. She could just see the cellar stairs. Then she heard another faint creak, and a shadow moved. There was someone standing there, standing still, watching and listening.

Suddenly a powerful torch beam flashed around the cellar. Andrea shut her eyes as it swept past her. She backed away, her heart hammering, and dived through another opening. Cobwebs clung to her face. She rolled and tumbled through another opening, and another, not caring now how much noise she made, desperate to get out. She could hear scrabbling behind her, and a muffled curse.

Now she could see the broken window. She scrambled onto the broken chairs and flung herself through the gap, falling heavily onto her hands and knees on the ground outside. She picked up her bag and started to limp away through the undergrowth.

'They're outside!'

It was a man's voice, coming from inside the house. She glanced back instinctively and saw a figure standing at a darkened upstairs window.

Andrea turned and ran for the gate. She scrambled through and tore down the lane and into the street.

She hurried on, her chest heaving, every breath painful. Her knee was bleeding. All the way home she kept looking over her shoulder to see if anyone was after her.

6

DAVID was disappointed. He'd been daydreaming about the tunnels all day, and the bus ride home had seemed interminable. Of course he was pleased that he had got into a selective school, and so were his parents, but sometimes he wished he could just walk up the road to the ordinary high school with kids he knew. His new friends weren't the kind to go mucking around in the park on the days when he still felt like breaking out and doing stupid things. Exploring that tunnel had been exceptionally stupid. He grinned at the thought of it. He would never have done it without Martin and Andrea to spur him on.

But there was no way he would want to go back in there with just Andrea. She was fun to be around, but he knew she didn't like him. That left Marty – who was grounded. Never mind, he must be able to take phone calls.

It was Kitty who answered. 'Hello, this is Kitty O'Brien.'

'Is Marty there?'

'David! You'll never guess what I've found out.' Kitty's voice faded to a conspiratorial whisper. 'I've met this lady . . . Haunted House . . . who the ghost is.'

'What? Speak louder, I can't hear you.'

He could hear Kitty's mother's voice in the background, then there was a long silence. At his end, classical music played while Moshe, his grandfather, rattled pots and pans in the kitchen.

'Hi,' came Martin's voice.

'Hi.'

'Andrea told you?'

'Yeah, she said you were grounded. What was Kitty going on about? I couldn't hear a word.'

'Tell you later.' Martin's voice was guarded. Clearly there were parents within earshot. 'Did you and Andrea have another look?'

'Uh – no, we both suddenly had other things to do. Anyway, when do you get out of jail?'

'The weekend, with good behaviour. Let's . . . umm . . . do what we were going to do then.'

'Yeah, make it Saturday afternoon.' Now it was David's turn to drop his voice. 'I need an excuse. My folks are at me to go to a residents' action meeting with them.'

Martin groaned. 'What is it this time?'

'Oh, that housing development they're trying to stop. Those meetings are so boring.'

'Sounds gruesome. Well, I get back from soccer about one. Come over then, okay?'

'Yeah. Great.'

David wandered into the kitchen.

'Ah! Looking for a job?' Moshe wanted company as much as a helper.

'Well . . .'

'You can top and tail these beans, if you like.'

Resigned, David pulled out a stool and sat at the big central bench.

'I mightn't make it to that meeting on Saturday,' he said as he worked. 'I might have to help Marty study for a big maths test.'

'Maths? Maybe I could help him,' said his grandfather.

David rolled his eyes. 'Moshe, we don't do maths your way any more. We use, like, calculators and stuff. No offence.'

'None taken,' said Moshe philosophically. 'I'm not so good at pressing buttons.'

David finished the beans. 'How long till dinner?'

'Quite a while,' said Moshe. 'Your mother's working late, your father's working late. We might have time for a game of chess.'

'Are you sure you can take the humiliation?' David went to the cupboard for the chess set.

'Ah, the boy's growing up! Maybe it's time for me to stop letting you win?'

'In your dreams, old man.'

As he exchanged knights and castles with his grandfather, David's mind wandered back to the mysterious tunnel system and its secret exit under the old house, and he wondered how the others felt about it. Marty was excited, he knew, but it was hard to tell with Andrea. She probably couldn't care less, he decided.

'Hmmm.' His grandfather's voice interrupted his reverie. 'I think you'll find that's checkmate.'

7

WHEN Kitty came out of school the next day, Andrea was waiting on the stone wall outside the gate. Rosa mumbled a farewell and retreated, running to catch up with another group.

'Did you get out early?' Kitty sat down next to Andrea.

'Nah. We had sport, so I jigged.'

'Did you and David go exploring yesterday?' asked Kitty.

'He didn't stick around, but I found a way into the house.' Andrea traced a pattern on the ground with her foot. 'It's really awesome, but I nearly got caught in there.'

'No way! Was it a ghost?'

'Course not, Kitty. It was some kind of security guys. I only just got away.' She frowned. 'It's a pity, 'cos I thought up this great plan. I thought I could run away from home and live there.'

'Why?'

'Maybe I could make a hidey-hole in the cellar and keep really quiet when they come round. Would you bring me extra food and stuff? You could leave it in the garden, and we could have a signal.'

'But Andrea, that sounds awful. Why do you want to run away?'

'Oh, I'm just sick of everything.' Andrea jumped up and started striding along the street. Kitty ran to catch up with her.

'What's wrong? What are you sick of?'

'Home. Mum. Celeste. School.'

'Are you in trouble again?'

'No, but we've got this really mean History teacher, Miss Tenniel. I don't know why she has to pick on me.'

'Miss Tenniel sounds nice. In Martin's mid-year report she said he had an active imagination.'

'Yeah, well, she's going to write to my dad if I don't do my assignment.'

'So?'

'My dad thinks I'm doing really great. I don't want some stupid teacher telling him lies about me.' Andrea's voice cracked.

'Why don't you just do your assignment?' asked Kitty.

'I'm going to run away.'

'What's it supposed to be, your assignment?'

'Don't be boring, Kitty! I'm not doing it, okay?'

'Just tell me!'

'It's some stupid thing for History,' said Andrea impatiently. 'Write about someone you know who's – sort of – been in history. Someone old, I suppose.'

Kitty danced around excitedly. 'But I can help you!'

'Yeah? You'll bring me things? You won't tell anyone where I am?'

'No, with your assignment. There's this old lady. She actually lived in the Haunted House, and before that in Christina Street, near your place, and there was the Depression . . . There's loads of history. She was in service, and the babies died. I've got my notes here.'

Andrea was shaking her head. 'It's too much work, I can't do it.'

'Yes you can!' Kitty was insistent. 'I'll help you. Oh, come on, Andrea, it'll be great. You'll be top of your class! You can show it to your dad. How long have you got?'

'I don't know – a few days.'

'Easy-peasy! Oh, this is perfect. We can go and see her now. Come on!'

'Where?' Andrea was obviously interested, in spite of her-self. 'Who is this person?'

'Miss Gordon – in the Sunset Home. I've already inter-viewed her, but I've thought of lots more questions, and she's really nice. Come on, I've just got to ask Mum, but she'll let me 'cos it's for school.'

Andrea frowned. 'Did you say she lived in the Haunted House?'

'Yeah, see? This is how we can find out about the house. Tarcoola, it's called. Did you know that? She was the mistress of Tarcoola, but she was poor before that. But Cec says some-one committed suicide in the house. He was a bigamist, you see. He's just got to be the ghost.'

'Hang on! Cec is a bigamist? How can Cec be the ghost?'

'No, no, not Cec. Mr Wolf! Andrea, you've really got to listen.'

Kitty quickly recounted her conversation with Miss Gordon, dragging her neatly written notes out of her schoolbag.

When they reached the O'Briens' house Andrea, who was convinced Kitty's parents didn't like her, waited outside. Kitty flew in and out like a boomerang, announcing to her startled mother that she was off to the Sunset Home and would be back in no time. She was afraid Andrea might not have waited, but when she got to the corner her friend came slouching out of a lane, looking around nervously.

'What about the tunnels?' demanded Andrea. 'Did the old girl say anything about them?'

'No, but she rambles on a bit,' said Kitty. 'If we listen carefully she might.'

'Maybe we could drop hints,' said Andrea.

'Well . . . maybe.' Kitty had her doubts about Andrea's hints. 'Just try not to make her suspicious, okay?'

The Matron of the Sunset Home was in the entrance hall when they arrived.

'Back again?' she said.

'Is it okay if I go and see Miss Gordon?' asked Kitty politely. 'The nurse said she likes having visitors.'

'Hmm. I suppose it won't hurt. And your friend?' The Matron's penetrating gaze swept over Andrea's torn leggings and layers of shredded tank tops in different colours.

Kitty could feel Andrea bristling a little beside her. 'This is Andrea McKinley-Brown,' she said hastily. 'She's doing some historical research for school as well.'

'I suppose that's all right, then,' said the Matron grudgingly. Kitty and Andrea ran up the stairs.

Miss Gordon was resting on her bed, propped up with pillows and gazing out the window. Kitty approached her shyly.

'Hello, Miss Gordon.'

'I've had my tea, thank you, dear.' Miss Gordon did not turn her head.

'It's me, Kitty.' She gently touched the old lady's hand. 'I've come back to visit you.'

Miss Gordon turned, and her face lit up. 'The nice little girl with all the questions!'

'That's right. You told me lots of interesting things. The only thing you wouldn't tell me was your date of birth.'

'The second of January, nineteen nineteen,' said Miss Gordon promptly. 'Right there in the front room at Christina Street, where Mother had all her babies.'

'Umm, I've brought a friend to meet you,' said Kitty. 'This is Andrea.'

'A friend?' The old lady looked Andrea up and down, seeming to take in every detail of her appearance, from her oddly cut hair to her mismatched socks. 'What's your name again, dear?'

'Andrea.'

'You have beautiful skin, Andrea. You must look after it. Always wash your face in cold water, and no soap.'

She looked away again. The light from the window fell obliquely on her face, heightening the shadows of her cheekbones and softening the lines and wrinkles. Andrea looked at her for a moment, then started scrabbling in her schoolbag.

'Andrea and I both have to do someone's life story, for school,' explained Kitty. 'Would you mind if we wrote about you? Mine has to be local history, you see.'

'Oh, you don't want to write about me. I was just a poor young thing. I never had an education, though I learnt a lot from Mr Wolf.'

Andrea produced a tattered photograph from her bag and held it up. 'Is this you?' she demanded.

Miss Gordon took the photograph. 'You found that old thing! Isn't it dreadful. I never took a good picture. Look, I wrote my name on the back.' She turned it over.

'I couldn't read that old-fashioned writing,' confessed Andrea.

'There's not much left of it,' said Miss Gordon. 'Or maybe it's my old eyes. But it says "Clarissa Gordon Wolf". That's me.'

Kitty looked over Miss Gordon's shoulder as she examined the photograph. It showed a young woman in a square-necked dress, her dark hair piled on her head.

'Oh, Miss Gordon, you were beautiful! And what a lovely dress!' She grabbed Andrea's elbow. 'Where did you get it?' she whispered.

'In the house,' Andrea whispered back.

Miss Gordon was still looking at the photograph.

'That was my cream silk. I had the finest clothes,' she sighed. 'I wonder what became of them? I suppose Mrs Wolf took them after the war. She took everything, then she let the house go to rack and ruin. Except my view. She couldn't take my view.'

'Who was Mrs Wolf?' asked Andrea.

'She waved those papers at me,' said Miss Gordon. 'She told me to get out, or she'd send lawyers. I know what Mr Wolf would have said to her lawyers.'

'So she was Mr Wolf's real wife?' asked Kitty gently.

'No! I was his wife. We had such a lovely wedding, and he took me to the Great Barrier Reef for our honeymoon. We went out on a boat.'

She sat up very straight and looked at them proudly.

'He made me feel like a real lady. If only they hadn't come, with the bombs.'

'What bombs?' asked Kitty.

'You remember the bombs, dear!' The faded blue eyes were wide. 'What a noise they made, all night long. I tried to tell him we were safe in the shelter, but I couldn't make him listen.'

There were tears in her eyes now. Kitty took the old lady's withered hand in one hand and stroked it with the other.

'I'm sorry,' she said. 'We didn't mean to upset you. We'll talk about something else if you like.'

'That's a good girl,' said Miss Gordon. 'You're both good girls. You're not from Tarcoola, are you?'

They shook their heads.

'They're good girls at Tarcoola, mind, but not very . . . I'm sorry to say this, but they're not very clever. If that Molly lets the stove go out she just cannot light it again. And I'd never let poor Lydia dust my room.'

Kitty rolled her eyes a little, but Andrea wasn't paying attention to her.

'That big room upstairs is yours, isn't it?' she said. 'With the view across the garden?'

'Don't go back there,' said Miss Gordon harshly, looking directly at her. 'That's not the place for you. Don't let the wolf boy catch you there.'

Andrea gasped.

Miss Gordon leaned forward. 'I'll tell Kitty where it is before I die,' she said in a hoarse whisper. 'We won't let the wolf boy get it. Kitty will look after it for me. Won't you, dear?'

Kitty felt tears prickling her eyelids. 'Yes! Yes, of course I will.'

'Good.' Miss Gordon lay back on her bed. In shadow, her face was gaunt. 'So nice to have seen you, dears.'

'Oh, yes.' Kitty jumped up. 'We have to go now.' Andrea opened her mouth to protest, but Kitty frowned fiercely at her. 'I'm sorry if we've tired you,' she added.

'Not at all, dear.' Miss Gordon took Kitty's hand and held it.

On an impulse Kitty leaned over and kissed her on the cheek.

'I'll come again soon,' she said.

Andrea approached the bed shyly and took Miss Gordon's hand. 'I'll come too, if I can,' she said. 'Should I leave the photo here?'

'No, keep it, dear. It's yours.' Miss Gordon touched Andrea's cheek. 'Goodbye. Be careful.'

'I will.'

The Matron was still in the hallway, deep in conversation with a balding man in a light-coloured suit. He turned to look as the two girls ran past and out into the sunlight.

'Well?' demanded Kitty. 'Do you see what I mean?'

'She's so sad!' said Andrea. 'So sad and so beautiful. And people were really mean to her.'

'People were strange in the old days,' agreed Kitty. 'But don't you think she would be great for your assignment?'

'But she went a bit gaga at the end,' frowned Andrea. 'Can we believe the things she says?'

'I don't know about the bombs and stuff, and she seems to go loopy when she's tired. But surely we can find out about Mr Wolf, and if he really killed himself.'

'Oh yeah. How?'

'I don't know, but I'll think of something,' promised Kitty, her eyes alight with the thrill of the chase.

8

SATURDAY arrived at last, and David slipped out of the house straight after lunch, leaving his mother on the phone making last-minute arrangements for the residents' action meeting. His father and Moshe were washing the dishes.

There were no cars outside Martin's house. David looked at his watch. It was not quite one o'clock.

Instead of sitting on the front step, he meandered along the street and around the corner, past the abandoned factory buildings. He strolled along the cyclone-wire fence, dragging his hand, feeling the ripples. A little breeze sighed in the trees by the old house.

David squinted at the development notice attached to a post in the grounds of the factory. It seemed a silly place to put a public notice, where it could hardly be seen from the street. He remembered his mother talking to people on the phone about the meeting. She had been describing something like this, talking about underhand dealings and saying that the Council ought to be investigated.

It struck him that this might be the development his parents had been droning on about. He racked his brains to remember some of what they had said. Yes, they had mentioned an old factory. And a lot of houses to be built – forty-something, maybe. The thought of the Haunted House surrounded by forty smart townhouses was ludicrous.

The factory gate was half off its hinges, with plenty of space to squeeze through. David ran down the rickety steps onto the glass-strewn asphalt and peered at the notice. It showed the site as an irregular shape divided into rectangles, each one presumably representing a house block. David looked around, trying to get his bearings. It would help, he thought, if the plan showed the Haunted House, or at least showed the direction of the park and the water. As it was, he couldn't make much sense of it.

The whole thing made him uneasy. If they cleaned up the factory site and built houses on it, would they leave the old house and the overgrown garden alone? Wouldn't the people who moved into the smart new houses complain, and want everything neat and tidy? He liked the garden the way it was, with its tangled undergrowth and hidden corners, snakes and all.

In fact – he looked again at the plan – where was the garden? Wouldn't it be shown somewhere in the drawing as a big open space? Little cogs started to click into place in his brain.

MARTIN answered the door, his mouth full.

'You look as if you've seen a ghost,' he mumbled.

'I just came by the Haunted House,' said David.

'You have seen a ghost!'

'Very funny.' David followed Martin into the little dining room. There were soup bowls and baguettes on the table, and Martin resumed eating as fast as he could.

'I have seen into the future,' said David gloomily. 'I don't suppose you've ever noticed that sign on the old factory site? The development notice?'

'Well, yeah. That's been there forever.'

'Did it cross your mind that it's the development people have been going on about?'

'Oh. Right.'

'I think they're going to take out the garden around the house, as well as the factory.'

'Yeah, but it'll be okay,' said Martin. 'Your parents and all those other people will stop it.'

'I hope so. My mum was talking about it on the phone just now. She said the developer guy owns half the council, and all his applications get through.'

'He's a bit of a crook, that Harold Buckingham,' said Martin's father, coming into the room with a pot of steaming soup. 'He had this lovely old house in Marrickville last year, heritage, and there was a preservation order on it. So he sent in bulldozers in the middle of the night. By the time the residents knew what was happening, there was nothing left to save.'

'But he wouldn't do that to the Haunted House?' Martin was horror-struck.

'Wouldn't put it past him.'

'But why would he want to demolish it?' asked David.

'Hey, you kids haven't been playing around there, have you?'

'No, Dad,' said Martin quickly.

'Well, make sure you don't. That old place has been neglected for years. It could be ready to fall down, for all I know.'

At that moment a key scraped in the lock and Kitty tumbled into the room, her eyes bright, spilling bags and parcels. Her mother followed.

'I've got my new shoes,' said Kitty. 'And we had lunch at Broadway. We went to that sushi train!'

Kitty's mother was already collecting plates. 'We'd better hurry, Paul,' she was saying. 'The movie starts at one forty-five.'

'You're going out?' asked Martin.

'Just to a movie, but we might call in on Marion and Steve afterwards. Will you kids be okay on your own?'

'Of course, Mum!' Martin and Kitty cried in unison.

'We might go to the park for a while,' added Martin.

'Well, make sure you lock up and take a key. And don't play around those cliffs!'

'We won't,' they chorused.

Finally the door slammed.

'All right!' shouted Martin, exchanging a high-five with David. 'Let's get going!'

'Wait a sec,' said Kitty. 'Andrea might be lurking outside. She was probably waiting for Mum and Dad to leave.'

Sure enough, Andrea was on the front verandah. She came in rather shyly.

'I've made a few preparations,' said David modestly. He opened the backpack he had brought.

'There's this.' He brought out a coil of new white rope. 'It's what climbers use,' he said. 'I've also got a knife, for marking our way, and – um – a torch.' He brought out a baseball cap with a torch duct-taped to its peak. Thin wires led from the torch to a pair of batteries, strapped together, which David also produced. He put the batteries in his pocket and the cap on his head.

'I do have a head-torch, but the beam's not wide enough,' he said. 'This is quite strong, because I've used extra batteries. I've rigged up a switch.'

He pressed a switch attached to another wire. The torch flickered on and off. David fiddled with the wires, frowning.

'Great!' said Martin politely, but Andrea burst out laughing.

'I'm sorry,' she spluttered. 'It's just . . . I'm sorry. I've got to get a picture of this.' She pulled a camera out of her bag and snapped.

'I don't know if it'll come out,' she said. 'I didn't want to use the flash. I'm saving the battery for the tunnels.'

'You're not taking a camera down there?' protested Martin.

'Why not?'

'It's . . . it's just wrong!' chimed in David.

'Why?'

'See, in role-playing games, the most unprepared person is a tourist,' Martin explained with unusual patience.

'A tourist?'

'Yes, a tourist goes exploring the dungeon with just a camera, instead of taking useful stuff, like . . . um . . . weapons.'

'Weapons,' said Andrea. 'Well, Marty, this isn't a role-playing game. This is reality, and I'm bringing a camera. What are you bringing?'

'Well, I'll be making a map, of course.' Martin took a notebook and a pencil from the top of the refrigerator. 'And I've been brushing up on my skills.' He made a few practice karate moves.

'I'm bringing some food,' said Kitty, busy opening cupboards. 'Someone help me with this stuff.' She piled some muesli bars, water bottles, apples and sultanas onto the table. They put some in David's backpack and some in an old schoolbag of Martin's.

'I've also got some candles,' contributed Andrea.

'Oh, great,' said David flatly. 'Any matches?'

Andrea produced a cigarette lighter.

'Now, before we get there,' started Kitty as they set off down the street, 'Andrea and I have to tell you all about Miss Gordon, the lady who used to live in the house.'

'Later,' said Martin impatiently, striding ahead.

'And listen,' interrupted Andrea. 'We have to be really careful when we get near the house, because . . .'

'But it's important!' Ignoring her, Kitty was trying to catch up with the boys. 'She said she was the mistress of Tarcoola, but Cec says the house has been empty since the war. Cec says someone committed suicide there! So there really is a ghost, but Miss Gordon—'

'Not now!' said David. 'Come on, let's take a shortcut through the factory.' He led the way to the gate at the top of the steps and they all slipped through the gap.

'See the sign?' said David. 'All of this is going! That bit must be where the Haunted House is now. I think your dad's right. I think they are going to pull it down.'

Andrea was dismayed. 'They can't pull down the Haunted House!' she said. 'Aren't there laws stopping them? Because it's – sort of – historical?'

'The only law around here is money,' said David.

'Well, let's explore it while we can,' said Martin, striding on.

They stepped over the low stone wall and approached the deserted house cautiously.

'We've got to be really quiet,' whispered Andrea. 'I came here the other day, but someone turned up – security guards or something. I nearly got caught.'

'That's all we need,' muttered David. 'To get arrested for trespassing.'

'But I found a good way to get in,' persisted Andrea. 'Do you want me to show you?'

'Later!' cried Martin and David together.

Martin ran to the corner of the house, peeped around, then gestured for the others to follow. David ran after him. It was kind of silly, but kind of fun. The two boys took turns scouting the area, making sure it was safe, then one by one they all climbed in through the broken window.

David stooped and ran through the cellar, and the others scrambled after him.

They pushed the wooden crates away from the trapdoor and climbed down the ladder. David crammed his cap onto his head, and the torch flashed on. Martin got out his pad and started drawing.

'We know where this door leads,' he said, indicating the entrance to the tunnel that led to the Doughnut. 'Though we might explore it some more later.'

'Why are you drawing those funny shapes?' demanded Kitty. 'This entrance shaft is square, and the doors in both those arches are rectangles. Why are you drawing them all as hexagons?'

'That's just the way it's done,' snapped Martin. 'Isn't it, Dave?'

'Sure,' said David. 'It's another role-playing game thing.'

He examined the heavy wooden door opposite. 'This one's well and truly locked,' he said. The door had a large, old-fashioned keyhole.

'Let's try one of these other tunnels, then,' said Andrea, plunging through one of the open archways.

'Wait!' said David, grabbing her arm. 'We've got to stick together. I think we should use the rope.'

'What, like mountaineers?' Andrea smiled. David was still holding her arm. She glanced down at his hand. He flushed and started fiddling with his pack, pulling out the rope.

'There could be holes in the floor,' he said. 'Or ... or anything.'

'He's right,' put in Martin. 'If we're tied together at least we can't lose anyone.'

'I'd better go first,' said David. 'I've got the torch.'

The two girls both looked at Martin. There was a dangerous glint in their eyes.

'I'll go last,' he said diplomatically. 'In case we're attacked from the rear,' he added.

'Right,' said David. Kitty rolled her eyes, and Andrea giggled.

When they were all tied together to David's satisfaction, they set off. The tunnel they chose seemed to have been hewn out of the sandstone. It was just wide enough and high enough for them to go through in single file, and it ran straight ahead for a few metres before opening into an irregularly shaped cave, about as big as a small room and sloping downwards at one end, where it narrowed again into another tunnel. They squeezed in. As they moved forward the unpleasant smell that hung around the entrance shaft faded. The air here was thin, faintly sour and damp.

The sloping tunnel became narrower and steeper, but then it widened again into a more regular shape, with rough stone steps going down.

'Do you want to know what I think?' said David.

'No!' the others chorused automatically.

'I think,' David went on, 'that some of these are natural

tunnels, but where they wouldn't join up properly someone's dug them out. Look!'

On their left as they descended the steps there was another opening. Here the wall was not rock but close-packed earth, and the rectangular tunnel was shored up with massive pieces of timber. It was about two metres wide, and high enough for an adult to walk through. They plunged into it eagerly, but after a short distance it petered out. A few spare lengths of timber lay at their feet, with an impenetrable earth wall in front.

'Well, they gave up on that one,' murmured Kitty.

'Looks like it.' David swept his torch in a wide arc as he led them back. Martin scribbled busily, adding hexagons to his incomprehensible map.

They continued downwards. There were more tunnels cut into the sides of the passage, much like the first one. None of them extended for more than twenty metres or so. One led them only a few metres into the earth before rubble and loose earth blocked their path. The massive beams of wood which had once held the tunnel's shape seemed to have collapsed into a splintered heap.

'I don't like the look of that,' said Andrea, a little shakily.

'I wonder when it happened?' Kitty said to no one in particular.

'Maybe we should stick to the stone tunnels,' said David. 'I think they might last longer.'

The passage led steeply downwards now, twisting and

turning. Suddenly David stopped short.

'What is it?' said Kitty, peeping over his shoulder. 'It hasn't caved in, has it?'

'No. Look!' David stepped forward and turned his head, so that his torch beam swept around a huge cave. It was so high the ceiling was lost in shadows. The floor was fairly level, but in the middle it reared up in great rocky projections, like a maze of graceful pillars.

'Cool!' said Andrea, pushing past the others. 'It's an underground palace!'

They wandered into the chamber.

'They're sort of like stalagmites,' said Kitty, stroking one of the pillars.

'Right,' said David. 'How do you remember which is which?'

'Stalagmites *might* just grow up to the roof, and stalactites have to hold on *tight*.'

'Oh, that's good. My grandfather taught me that stalagmites have a G for *ground*, and stalactites have a T for *top*.'

Andrea took several photographs, the flash lighting up the cave. The walls were honeycombed in places. Some of the hollows were obviously shallow, but many of them extended into darkness.

'That's it,' she murmured. 'I'd better not drain the battery.'

Martin was having some difficulty working on his map in the erratic light. Then he dropped a bombshell.

'Umm, does anyone remember exactly where we came in?' he asked casually.

9

DAVID opened and shut his mouth a few times, but nothing came out.

'I thought you were making a map,' he said finally.

'Yeah, but . . .' Martin looked intently at his map. Andrea looked over his shoulder.

'It doesn't give much away, does it?' she remarked.

'Well, what about your knife, and marking our way?' Martin said accusingly to David.

'I was going to, but you were all rushing around taking photographs.' He glared meaningfully at Andrea. 'Being tourists.'

'Let's have something to eat,' said Kitty brightly.

'All right, but we'd better get untied first,' conceded Andrea.

They freed themselves and attacked the food, which Kitty had laid out on a flat rock.

'Don't eat it all!' she warned. 'We may have to go onto rations.'

Andrea scratched around in her bag and produced a candle which she balanced on the rock and lit. In the flickering light her face was ghostly. Kitty shivered.

'There's something about this place,' she said. 'We're not supposed to be here.'

David wandered around with the torch, trying to find the opening through which they had entered.

'Look,' he said, coming back to the others. 'I've found a possibility. I've made a mark there, anyway. We'll just have to have a look.'

'Okay.' Martin threw away his apple core.

'Martin!' Kitty's voice was stern. 'Bring that back here.'

'All right, Mum.' He retrieved the apple core and put it in the bag.

'Aren't we going to get tied up again?' demanded Andrea.

'Oh – I suppose we'd better.' David untangled the rope and tied it on securely, passing the end to Andrea. She did a double knot around her waist and passed it to Kitty and Martin.

'Let's leave the candle burning here,' Andrea suggested.

They moved cautiously into the tunnel David had chosen. He started to have doubts almost immediately. It felt a little too narrow, and wound a little too tightly. Then suddenly it was broader and flatter.

'Sorry,' said David. 'Definitely not it.'

Martin pushed forward to look. 'There wasn't a wide bit, was there?'

'No, and it's very rough on the ground now.' David looked down, and his torch swept over rocks and loose stones. 'I don't like this. Let's go back.'

He turned towards Andrea, and stumbled. A rock rolled under his foot, pitching him into the wall of the tunnel. The rope jerked, pulling Andrea off balance. There was a rumble and, with a flurry of loose stones, the ground opened up beneath her. Andrea screamed and disappeared.

The rope snapped tight around David's waist and his legs were jerked from under him. Face-down, scrabbling for something to cling to as Andrea's weight and momentum dragged him backwards, he could see nothing but a blur of rocks and stones on the ground beneath him. Then his torch went out.

He could hear dragging and scrabbling noises from the other side of the hole. Kitty was screaming 'Andrea!' and Martin was screaming 'Kitty!' Were they all sliding into the hole?

David managed to hook his arm around a rock that was not loose and the rope jerked tight around his waist. He could hardly breathe. He fumbled with his free hand for the switch.

'Don't let me go!' called Andrea's plaintive voice.

'Can you grab hold of something?' David said, straining to turn on the torch.

'No!' She was obviously squirming around. The rope tightened around David's waist. 'There's nothing here. Where's the light?'

Finally David flashed on the torch to reveal Martin and Kitty opposite. They were standing rigid and locked together, straining back against the rope.

'How long do we have to hold on?' asked Martin, looking up at the light.

David swivelled his head. Between them, the floor had completely given way, leaving a hole about two metres across.

The torch beam caught Andrea's pale face as she dangled in the middle.

'Do you think you can pull her up?' called David.

'Not while she's tied to you,' said Martin.

'Get me out of here!' pleaded Andrea.

'Shut up!' snapped David. 'I'm thinking.' The rock was cutting into his arm. 'Look, I'll have to cut the rope,' he said.

'No!' screamed Andrea.

'No, listen!' insisted David. 'We can't all pull you up. We'd be pulling in different directions. Martin, are you sure you and Kitty can take the weight?'

'It's the only way,' said Martin. 'What do you think, Kit?'

'Come on,' said Kitty. 'Let's just do it.'

David groped for his knife, found it and sawed at the rope. It was difficult, because the rope was strong and the knife fairly blunt. At last he felt the fibres giving way.

'Get ready!' he called. 'It's going!'

He heard Andrea give a little gasp as the rope snapped, and the rattle of stones falling past her. Kitty and Martin dug in their heels and held on grimly as she thudded against their side of the hole.

'Have you got her?' David flashed the torch.

'Yes!' Martin was breathless. 'Pull, Kitty!'

Slowly, agonisingly they edged backwards. Scrabbling sounds came from inside the hole. David came as close to the edge as he dared and shone the torch to guide Andrea as she scrambled for handholds. At last she pulled herself up and lay panting on the rocks.

'Keep going!' urged David. 'The edge might give way.' Andrea hastily crawled forward and joined Martin and Kitty, who had also sunk to the ground, weak with relief.

With shaking fingers David untied the rope from around his waist. He could still feel the pain where it had cut in.

'Is everyone okay?' he asked.

'Yeah. Thanks,' said Andrea.

David stood up and directed his torch beam into the gaping hole.

'Have a look at this!' he said unsteadily.

The others edged closer to the hole and peered in. The torch beam travelled down through darkness. Far below, a few tumbled rocks reflected the faint light.

'I think I'm going to throw up,' announced Andrea.

'Wait a minute,' said Martin. 'Can't you keep it still, Dave? There's something down there.'

David held the torch as steadily as he could. Something glinted at the foot of the shaft.

'See that?' said Martin. 'It's . . . like railway lines. Why would there be railway lines down here?'

'Look,' interrupted David, 'I hate to spoil the party, but I've got a bit of a problem here. Like where do I go now?'

He raised the torch and swept it around the edges of the hole. The whole floor of the tunnel between him and the others had collapsed, and there was obviously no way for him to climb back.

'Maybe there's a way out on your side,' suggested Kitty.

'I'll have a look.' David turned and shone his torch along the passage.

'Hey, don't leave us in the dark!' Andrea cried.

'Light one of your candles, then.'

Andrea groped in her bag, found a candle and lit it. The shadows flickered eerily.

David set off uneasily, testing the floor with every footstep. He didn't have to go far to find the tunnel blocked by a big rock-fall.

'Can't get through that way,' he announced, coming back. 'Not on my own. There's about a tonne of rock.'

'Can we find some wood?' suggested Kitty. 'Maybe we could make a bridge?'

'There's no wood.' David had already made up his mind. 'I'm going to jump across the gap.'

'No, David, don't,' said Martin. 'We'll go back and get help.'

'It makes sense,' said David. 'I can do it easily.'

'Let's use the rope somehow,' insisted Martin. 'We can pull you across . . .'

'If it was you, you'd jump,' said David.

There was a silence.

'Wouldn't you?'

'Maybe, but . . .'

'But Martin won the long jump at the sports carnival!' said Kitty.

'Well, so he did.' David didn't quite succeed in keeping the tremor out of his voice. 'I don't think I went in that event. About four metres, wasn't it, Marty?'

'Four point four eight, actually,' said Martin reluctantly.

'Right. Well, I'll need some light. Have you got any more candles?'

Andrea set up all her candles along the sides of the tunnel and across the edge of the hole and lit them solemnly. Kitty retreated back along the passage a little and sat down with her head on her knees. David moved to the edge of the hole and measured the distance across with his eyes, then paced out his run-up, counting.

'You won't be able to see the edge on your side.' Andrea's voice quavered.

'I can see it a bit. And I know how many steps.' David kept his voice steady. 'Now, get back and give me room.'

Martin and Andrea backed along the passage to join Kitty. David turned the torch off and waited for a moment until his eyes were used to the candlelight. He could see their shadowy outlines ahead of him, his goal. Then he was running, his footsteps thundering in the confined space.

Kitty still had her hands over her eyes when he fell forward, gasping, almost on top of them.

'Not too shabby!' Martin was grinning from ear to ear.

'My takeoff could have been better,' said David shakily. 'Do you think I should have another go?'

Kitty burst into tears. Andrea put an arm around her. The two boys blew out the candles and collected them all, then, with David's torch leading the way again, they made their way back to the vast cave.

'Now all we have to do is find the right entrance,' said David.

'Let's get into line, the way we were when we came in,' suggested Kitty.

'What good will that do?' scoffed Martin.

'You'll see.' They lined up, David first, followed by Kitty, Andrea and Martin.

'Now, we'll walk around the wall until we find a passage that looks right,' said Kitty.

'I think it's that one over there,' Andrea pointed.

They shuffled over to the opening.

'Let's pretend we're just coming out of this passage,' said Kitty. 'Turn around, David.'

They got into position. David swept the torch beam around.

'Oh, I see,' said Andrea. 'Those pillar things are too far to the left. They were more in front of us, weren't they? This is a good idea, Kitty.'

They worked their way around the wall until they found an entrance which seemed to be the right one.

'This is it!' said Martin. 'You're a genius, Kit!'

'I know,' said Kitty modestly, following David into the tunnel. He stopped after a few steps, and she bumped into his back. 'Ouch!'

'Sorry, genius,' said David. 'No go.' He shone his torch onto a solid stone wall in front of him.

'Never mind,' said Andrea. 'We're getting closer.'

After a few more false starts they found the way out. When they were sure of it, David went back and used his knife to scratch a big cross and an arrow by the entrance.

'Now, let's get the ropes on again,' he said.

The others nodded vigorously, and they roped themselves together, checking the knots carefully. David led the way back along the passage to the shaft.

'Umm, where to now?' he asked.

'I wouldn't mind getting out of here for a while,' confessed Martin. 'I could do with some fresh air.'

'Yes,' agreed Kitty. 'We can have a picnic in the garden with the rest of the food.'

They climbed up the shaft and made their way out of the cellar and into the garden of the Haunted House. The shadows were surprisingly long, but they found a sunny spot by a pond choked with water-lilies.

Andrea put her bag down, sat down on the edge of the pond and dabbled her hands in the greenish water.

'I'm starving,' she said. 'Have you got any more of those muesli bars?'

'Andrea!' gasped Kitty, staring at her. 'Your legs!'

Andrea's bare legs were streaked with blood from numerous cuts and scratches, and bruises were starting to develop. She held up her hands. Her fingers and wrists were a mess, covered with scratches.

'It hurt when I was climbing out of the hole,' she said. 'But then I forgot.'

'Come back to our place,' suggested Kitty. 'We've got some stuff to put on it, and bandaids . . .'

'Nah, I'm all right. Mum's got some herbal stuff at home. I'll have a long, hot bath.'

They finished the food.

'Are we coming back tomorrow?' asked David.

'You bet,' said Martin.

'We can't,' Kitty reminded him. 'We're going to the Blue Mountains to see our cousins.'

'Oh, why does that have to be tomorrow?' groaned Martin.

'Well, I'll be back,' announced Andrea. 'What about you, David? Are you up for it?'

'Oh! Yeah, sure. How about eleven o'clock?'

'Yep. Meet you in the garden at eleven.'

'But you'll see everything without us,' protested Kitty.

'We'll just have a little look,' David promised her. 'I can't spend too much time. I've got to make a model for Science.'

'And I've got a History assignment,' said Andrea.

The boys looked at her with surprise.

'So?' she said challengingly. 'So?'

'Fine,' said Martin. 'Fine.'

THEY separated at David's front gate. He let himself in and quietly stowed his backpack in the hall cupboard.

Cooking sounds were coming from the kitchen. His mother

had vegetables strewn over the bench and was frowning into the screen of her laptop.

'The recipe says chervil,' she said. 'I wonder if Italian parsley would do?'

David's heart sank a little. His mother's cooking was sometimes rather experimental. He preferred weekdays, when his grandfather took over.

'Can I help with dinner?' he offered.

'That would be lovely, darling. It says the potatoes have to be cut into two-centimetre cubes.' She pushed a board and a knife towards him, and he perched on a stool beside her.

'So how was the meeting?' he asked casually.

'Curiouser and curiouser,' murmured his mother. 'Is there something I'm missing? Or rather, something you're missing? Some new piece of technology you're hankering after?'

'No, Mother, I'm just interested.'

'Well, since you ask, there's a little light on the horizon today. I won't fill you in on all the details, for fear of sending you to sleep, but there's a bit of a legal hitch at the developer's end.'

'What kind of hitch?'

'Just the faintest possibility that the developer can't prove ownership. This guy, Harold Buckingham, is supposed to have inherited the property, but he can't produce any paperwork. It's all deliciously Dickensian. Original title deeds, signed and sealed with wax. Haven't been seen for sixty years.'

'So he can't go ahead?'

'Oh, he'll find them eventually, I suppose. But it gives us

a bit more time to get our case together, and with luck get a preservation order on the house.'

'Are they really going to wreck the house and the garden?'

'I'm afraid that's their plan. We're arguing that they should keep the garden and restore the house, turn it into apartments. But I think greed will prevail. He'll make a staggering amount of money.'

David pictured the precious document, yellow and tattered, rolled up into a scroll and tied with faded ribbon. Places like the Haunted House had secret passages and sliding panels. Maybe it was there, hidden somewhere. If he found it he would make sure Buckingham never got hold of it. Of course, he could never tell his mother. She was very strict on the law.

'David?'

'Sorry?'

'I said, how did you go with Martin today? Weren't you helping him with his maths?'

'Oh! Sure, he's fine. We hung out a bit in the park, too.'

'Good. Nothing like a bit of fresh air.'

David thought guiltily of the musty smell in the tunnels and the foul air in the shaft. Deeper down it smelled damp and earthy, like mushrooms. Most of all, he remembered the smokiness of Andrea's candles as he jumped.

'Yeah,' he said. 'It was good.'

10

ANDREA sat cross-legged on her narrow bed, copying Kitty's notes into an exercise book. It was cloudy outside, and not much early-morning light found its way into the room. She tried turning on her bedside lamp.

'Aarrgghhhh!' Celeste half sat up, platinum hair sticking out, and waved a protesting hand. She had come in noisily just before dawn, smelling of alcohol and cigarette smoke, and Andrea hadn't been able to get back to sleep.

Andrea turned off the lamp and took her things out to the kitchen. Dirty dishes were piled high on the bench and in the sink. Her mother was at the table, reading yesterday's paper and tapping cigarette ash into a half-empty coffee cup.

'Hello, love. I was just going to make some toast. Want some?'

'Okay. Thanks, Mum.'

Andrea slipped her books into her schoolbag, which lay on the floor by the door.

'I'm glad you're up, sweetie. We need to get stuck into that bathroom. It's a pigsty.'

Andrea sighed. Her mother hadn't stirred, so she dug out some bread and put it into the toaster.

DRESSED in leggings to cover her bruises and an old baggy jumper that she had found under Celeste's bed, Andrea helped her mother do a quick house-clean. As soon as they had finished she mumbled an excuse and left the house.

It was cold outside, with a biting wind. She slipped through the fence of the Haunted House and followed a faintly discernible brick-paved path through the overgrown garden, ducking her head to avoid overhanging branches.

The path led to a semi-circular walled garden filled with thorny rosebushes and edged with trees. In front of the trees was a broken pedestal on which stood a white stone statue of a naked woman, her long hair flowing around her shoulders, her eyes downcast. There were piles of rubble around the base of the pedestal, but the woman was intact.

Andrea folded her hands and looked down, unconsciously imitating the statue's pose.

Faintly, in the distance, she heard the town hall clock begin to strike.

She found her way through to the big stagnant pond and stopped some distance from it. David was sitting on its edge, skimming stones over the greenish water. A huge goldfish popped up its head, looked around in goggle-eyed surprise, then disappeared.

'Oh! Sorry, fishy,' said David, laughing. He tossed another stone into the pond.

'Talking to the fishes?' called Andrea.

'Yeah, if I say the magic words it'll turn into a frog.'

'Come and see what I've found.' Andrea led the way back to the rose garden and the white lady. 'Isn't she beautiful?'

She pulled her camera out of her bag. 'She's sort of like Sleeping Beauty, with all those briars.'

'Mmmm.' David looked embarrassed.

'Think of it as art, David!' exclaimed Andrea, laughing. 'Come on! I reckon we can get through here.'

They found a path that led to another statue in the middle of a round pond, now quite dry. This statue was a small boy, also naked, peeing into the pond. He was surrounded by fish with their mouths open, and the whole construction was clearly designed as a fountain. Some of the fish were broken, and the boy was missing an arm.

'More art!' said David, grinning.

Another path curved towards the open space in front of the house.

'Wait!' said Andrea. 'We don't have to climb through the window any more. I just have to find it . . .'

She led the way round another corner. This wall of the house faced the garden, and there were several glass doors.

'It's one of these . . .' She ran along, peering through dusty glass and trying door handles. 'Ah, here it is!'

The door swung stiffly inwards.

'What did you do?' asked David.

'I unlocked it from the inside last time I was here. Come in.'

They shut the door quietly and made their way through the house and down into the dark central area of the cellar. From there they found the trapdoor quite easily. At the bottom of the shaft, David donned his miner's cap and adjusted the torch.

'Pooh, that smell's bad today!' said Andrea, joining him.

'Yeah. Have you brought a torch?'

'Well, no, but I've made a holder for my candles, so the wax won't drip on my hand.'

She showed him the cone-shaped object with a rim, like an upside-down witch's hat, that she had made from cardboard; then she fitted a new white candle into the holder and flicked her cigarette lighter.

There was a faint whoooosh, and a huge blue-tinged flame leapt up.

'Turn it off!' cried David, but Andrea had already snapped the lighter shut. There was an acrid smell of burning hair.

'Is my hair on fire?' Andrea was close to panic.

'No, it's not burning.' David touched the soft thick hair that fell over her forehead. 'Some of the ends feel kind of hard and bristly. I think it's singed.'

'Arrrgh! It could've just burst into flame!' Andrea was a bit shaky. 'What on earth happened?'

'I don't know, but it's something to do with that smell. Let's see if the air's fresher in those other tunnels.'

Apart from the tunnel they had originally discovered, leading to the beach, and the locked door opposite, there were two more openings: the tunnel they had explored the day before, where Andrea had fallen into the hole, and another facing it.

'Looks like this is the one to try,' said David.

'I don't know,' said Andrea. 'I'd rather go back and have another look at that big cathedral cave.'

'Let's split up, then,' suggested David calmly.

'Okay.' Andrea prepared her candle, reached for the cigarette lighter again, and hesitated.

'Maybe I'll have a quick look at your one first,' she offered.

David led the way. The tunnel opened out almost immediately into a small, roundish cave with a narrow opening to one side. David flashed his torch into the opening.

'Look, someone's built all this,' he whispered. The rock sides were flat, and the roof of the tunnel was shored up with massive beams.

After only a few metres they stepped into another, larger cave.

'Eureka!' said David.

'Wow!' said Andrea, reaching for her camera.

The cave was roughly rectangular, and about the size of a large room. There was a patterned rug on the floor, grey with dirt and dust, and around the walls were cupboards, bookshelves, small tables and chests of drawers. At one end, behind a Japanese screen, were two beds made up with white sheets and thick grey blankets. There was a low table between the beds. On it stood a lamp and some books and newspapers.

The centre of the room was occupied by a long table. There were candles on the table, a few plates, none too clean, and an empty wine bottle.

David examined the bottle. 'Hmmm. Nineteen thirty-nine.

My dad'd kill for something like this!'

'So would mine,' said Andrea. She was busy lighting the candles. In their light the room was warm and welcoming.

David browsed through the bookshelves. As he pulled out each book, a cloud of dust rose and hovered in the air.

'Some of these are in German,' he said. 'I know this one – my grandfather has it. When my great-grandmother was still alive they used to read it to each other and cry.'

'Let's see.' Andrea peered over his shoulder. '*Faust.* My Dad's got something like this. In English, though.'

Everything in the cave was covered with a thick layer of dust. Andrea wandered around, opening cupboards and sneezing. She found several tins of food, some of them unlabelled and dulled with time, but some with modern labels and familiar brand names. There was a large wooden barrel with a tap. Andrea found a cup and poured out a few drops of clear fluid. She dipped a finger into it and tasted.

'Careful!' said David.

'It's just water,' she returned. 'Doesn't taste too bad. A bit woody.'

David took the cup and sniffed. 'A suggestion of oak on the nose,' he agreed gravely. He sipped. 'And definitely too much tannin in the aftertaste.'

Andrea giggled. 'Does your dad talk like that?'

'No, Roger Mason, our next-door neighbour. He runs that antique shop in Darling Street. He's always bringing in bottles of wine for my parents to taste with him. He's one of those people who know everything about everything.'

'Is he the man who gives those history lectures?'

'Yeah, that's him. He writes books and sells them in his shop, and takes people for historical walks.'

'Don't tell him about this place!' said Andrea.

'Never.' David resumed his exploration of the room.

'There's another tunnel over here!' he called. 'Oh no, sorry, it's just a sort of alcove.' He disappeared with his torch into a narrow cleft. There was a silence. Andrea stood alone in the centre of the cave, in the flickering candlelight. Faint scraping and rustling noises came from the alcove.

'David?' Andrea's voice quavered. Suddenly a creature leapt out of the cleft, flailing its arms. It had huge blowfly eyes and a long black snout. Andrea screamed.

'I'm going to get you!' announced the creature in a hollow voice.

'David, you rat! What is that thing?'

'Don't you know a gas mask when you see one?'

'Wow! It's the real deal, isn't it?'

She took a quick photograph before he pulled off his disguise.

'There are a few more in there,' he said. 'I know what this place is now.'

'What?'

'It's a bomb shelter.'

'What, nuclear fallout and stuff?'

'Could be, but I'm not sure. Nuclear fallout's fairly recent, isn't it? This place seems to be older than that.'

'Wait a minute,' said Andrea. 'Bomb shelter? The old lady said something about bombs.'

'What old lady?'

'The one Kitty keeps trying to tell you about. The one who lived in this house. She said there were bombs in the war. I think she might have said something about a shelter.'

'That sort of makes sense. These could be World War Two gas masks.'

'Oh, you'd know, would you?' scoffed Andrea.

'I've seen a few documentaries. TV's not all game shows, you know.'

Andrea chose to ignore him. She wandered into the alcove, selected another gas mask and tried it on.

'Yuk,' she said. 'It smells horrible.'

'Better than nerve gas,' said David. He sat down on one of the beds, producing a cloud of dust, and picked up the yellowed newspaper on the low table next to it.

'Hey, guess what. There's an ad here for the first Harry Potter movie.'

'That's funny.' Andrea came over to look. 'See the date? 2005!'

'I don't get it,' said David, looking around. 'The house is supposed to have been empty since the war. So who's been down here?'

'Whoever it was,' said Andrea cheerfully, 'they haven't been here for a while. Look at all the dust. And they left in a hurry,' she added. 'They didn't even wash up!' She picked up one of the plates from the table. It had faint smears of an unrecognisable substance.

'Yeah.' David looked uncomfortable. 'Did you say something yesterday about men in the house?'

'I reckon they were security guards, doing their rounds. One came down to the cellar with a torch and nearly caught me. And when I got out there was another one upstairs, looking out the window.'

'And you think they saw you?'

'When I was in the cellar the torch went right over my face. I don't know what he saw. Then when I got outside I just ran. It was pretty dark.'

'We'd better be careful.'

'We'll just stay away from the front door.' Andrea wandered around the room. The house and the figure with the torch didn't seem so scary now that she had company.

'Maybe we'll keep using the window in the cellar. It's more out of the way.' David moved towards the entrance.

'You don't want to go already, do you?' asked Andrea, dismayed.

'Well, I've got a lot of homework. You can stay if you like.'

'Okay,' said Andrea. 'I will.' She sat down at the table.

David turned on his torch.

'Don't use your candles in that shaft, though,' he said. 'If you catch fire I won't be here to save you.'

'Oh. Right.' Andrea sat doggedly at the table. 'Bye.'

'Bye.' David walked past her to the entrance. She sat calmly with her back to him. 'See you, then.'

'See you.' She didn't turn her head. She sat very still for a while, staring into space.

When she was quite sure David had gone she leaned over and blew out the candles on the table. In the faint light of her own candle, she went as far as she dared back towards the shaft.

'He could have waited,' she muttered crossly to herself. But at the same time she was glad David had assumed she wasn't scared of staying underground by herself. At least that showed some sort of respect. Maybe.

The smell grew stronger as she got closer to the shaft. Her candle flared up, and a shadow loomed menacingly on the wall in front of her. Andrea gasped and shrank back. The shadow shrank too.

Andrea looked around carefully, then blew out her candle. It was quite dark now, and her heart was pounding. She moved slowly, groping her way out. David had left the trapdoor open, so there was some illumination as she climbed the ladder. Trembling with relief, she scrambled up towards fresh air and freedom.

11

MARTIN spotted Andrea eating lunch with Tammy and Michelle. They were sitting on a patch of grass, skirts pushed up to get the maximum amount of sun on their winter-white legs. Shouts and the thump of a ball could be heard from the nearby basketball courts, and the warm breeze brought a whiff of cigarette smoke from a little hollow behind them.

Andrea's friends started whispering behind their hands as Martin approached.

'My sister wants you to meet her at the Balmain library,' he said gruffly.

'Oh, yeah?' said Michelle, raising an eyebrow.

'If you want to see Andrea, just say so,' advised Tammy. 'She won't bite you.' Both girls giggled.

Martin scowled and walked away. Andrea picked up her things and followed him down the steps towards the playing fields.

'I don't know why I hang out with them,' Andrea muttered.

Martin said nothing. It was a mystery to him too. Andrea had told Kitty that she hated Tammy and Michelle, but she spent a lot of time laughing and giggling in the school grounds with them, acting as if they were her best friends.

'What's this about the library?' asked Andrea.

She brushed some leaves off a bench and sat down. Martin sat next to her, not too close, and took his lunch out of his bag. A few seniors were kicking a ball around on the grassy oval. Beyond them the Harbour sparkled in the sunlight.

'Kitty wants you to meet her there after school. She thinks they might have old newspapers that'll tell you when some guy killed himself. I don't know what that's got to do with anything. She said it was because of bombs in the war, but that wouldn't have happened here, in Australia, would it? And why would it make someone kill himself?'

'I don't know,' said Andrea. 'This old lady of Kitty's, Miss Gordon, is pretty rambly, but she said there were bombs, and yesterday David and I found this amazing bomb shelter under the house. It's got food, and blankets, lots of really old stuff, and gas masks!'

'Wow! Any weapons?'

'No, Martin.'

'Anyway,' said Martin. 'Doesn't it show that she and this "What's the time, Mr Wolf" were both crazy right from the start? They'd have to be, like, paranoid to want a bomb shelter, wouldn't they?'

'It is weird. I mean, Australia's never been invaded.'

'Why don't we ask Miss Tenniel?' suggested Martin.

'Oh, sure.'

'Yeah, go and ask her. It's for your assignment, isn't it?'

'Enough already!' shouted Andrea. 'Why is everyone on my back about that stupid assignment?'

'Okay, okay!' Martin put up his arms as if to fend her off.

'I just want to find out more about the house,' said Andrea emphatically. 'The house, right?'

'All right, all right.'

There was a silence for a while.

'We could still ask Miss Tenniel,' said Martin hopefully.

'I'm not going to the staffroom. Someone might see me!' Andrea took a banana out of her bag and started to peel it. 'You ask Miss Tenniel.'

'Hey, it's not my assignment!' said Martin cheekily. Andrea beat him about the head and shoulders with her banana until he pleaded for mercy.

'Now look what you've done to my banana!' she cried.

'I'll have it. I like them mushy.'

'Oh yuk, Marty!' She watched him eat it. 'Anyway, what did you do your assignment on?'

'My great-grandpa. He used to have a farm up past Bathurst, but there was the Depression and a big drought, and he had to go on the wallaby.'

'On the what?'

'You know, being a swagman. I wrote five pages, with footnotes.'

'You don't have to do that much!'

'My parents get all keen, and they hang around and say

"Put this in" and "Put that in". You don't know how lucky you are. If I missed doing an assignment I'd be grounded for the rest of my life.'

'Poor you.' Andrea scuffled her feet on the ground. 'So when are you going to see Miss Tenniel?'

'What's it worth?' grinned Martin.

'I've got a bag full of mushy bananas at home.'

They went to the staffroom together. Andrea stepped back out of sight as Mr Blythe, the head of History, opened the door.

'It's a boy,' he said in his lugubrious voice. 'Go away, Boy.' He began to close the door.

Martin could see Miss Tenniel at her desk in a corner. He waved frantically. After a moment she came out, smiling.

'What can I do for you, Martin?'

'I just wanted to ask you something, Miss. About history.'

'Is it more medieval stuff? Knights and castles?'

'Not this time. It's about – um – World War Two.'

'Yes?'

'Well – our side won, didn't it?'

'Yes, of course. If you can say anyone ever wins a war.'

'So have we ever been bombed?'

'Oh, no. Well, I mean yes. Darwin was bombed. And Broome.'

'But what about here? Has Sydney ever been bombed?'

'Well – there were some submarines. I think they blew up a ship in the Harbour.'

'They did?' Martin's eyes lit up. 'When was that, Miss?'

'I couldn't tell you for sure. Let's see . . .' Miss Tenniel's eyes took on a faraway look. 'It must have been fairly early. Late forty-one maybe? No, it was after Darwin.' She put her head back inside the staffroom door and called above the hubbub inside. 'When were those Japanese mini-subs in the Harbour?'

Mr Blythe's voice boomed out: 'May thirty-first, nineteen forty-two. Send that boy away, Miss Tenniel. Mr King has made some magnificent coffee and I propose that we enjoy it.'

12

KITTY marched into the Balmain library and looked around. There were a few pensioners dozing over magazines in the lounge chairs and some older kids clustered around the computers. Kitty checked her watch. She wandered around the shelves for a few minutes, then went outside again and looked up and down the street. Finally she spotted Andrea lurking in the bushes.

'What are you doing there?' Kitty hissed. 'Come on, I haven't got much time.'

'I can't go in,' Andrea said sullenly. 'I've lost my card. Anyway, I got some books out once and never brought them back.'

'Don't be silly,' said Kitty. 'You don't have to borrow. We're just looking for information.'

'They might recognise me.'

'Course they won't. You were probably about six the last time you came here.'

The librarian was deep in conversation with some middle-aged ladies. Kitty waited patiently to be noticed while Andrea pretended to browse at a nearby shelf.

'I was wondering if you keep old newspapers,' said Kitty.

'How old?'

'I was looking for the local paper, from World War Two?'

'I'm not sure if there was one that long ago.' She tapped on the computer in front of her for a while. 'No. There've been a few different local papers over the years, but there wasn't one for this specific area during the war.'

'Oh. Where can we find out about local history, then? Stuff about local families, and . . . and things that might have happened to them?'

'We don't keep any real source material here. You'd have to go to the main library, at Leichhardt. They might be able to help you.'

'Thank you.' Kitty was crestfallen. She moved away from the desk.

'See?' said Andrea. 'It's just too complicated.'

'Right, you win. I give up,' snapped Kitty.

She walked out of the library and down the street, tears prickling her eyelids. She imagined Andrea stalking off in the opposite direction, but a moment later she felt a hand on her arm.

'Sorry,' muttered Andrea.

'It's okay.'

'So,' said Andrea. 'We'll just have to go to Leichhardt, right?'

'It's not that easy. Mum would never let me.' She cheered up all the same. Her brain was already at work, weighing up her chances.

She approached it casually while helping to make dinner.

'Mum, did you know all the local history stuff is in the Leichhardt library now?'

'Well, I suppose that makes sense. It's kind of central.' Her mother handed her some tomatoes to cut up.

'There's some information there I need. You know, for my project.'

'Oh Kitty, I wouldn't have time to take you to Leichhardt this week. Maybe on Saturday . . .'

'Mum, I could just get the bus after school. Straight there and straight back.'

'On your own? I don't think so.'

'If I get into a selective school next year I'll have to go on the bus.'

'We'll worry about that when it happens.'

Kitty slid the tomato pieces into the salad bowl, considering her options. Well, nothing to lose, she thought.

'What if I go with someone else?'

'Who?'

'Well . . . Andrea?'

'Andrea?' Her mother nearly dropped the pot she was carrying. 'Are you still hanging around with her?'

'Mum, you like Andrea, remember?'

'Yes, but Kitty. As she gets older, you know . . . she . . .'

Kitty was prepared for this. 'Mum, she's not a bad influence on me,' she said firmly. 'I'm a good influence on her.'

'All right,' said her mother, recognising a match point when she saw it. 'But all the same, you're not going to Leichhardt on the bus with Andrea or anyone else except me or some other parent, and that is final.'

13

KITTY sat at the dining-room table, working on her project. It was just amazing how much information had come out of one little interview. Now that David and Andrea had found the shelter, and Martin had discovered that there really were bombs, she was determined to follow up every single thing Miss Gordon had said. Andrea had better not have given up on the idea of going to Leichhardt. Martin was printing all her photos right now, two copies, and Kitty would have to pay by doing his share of the washing-up for three days.

She thought of Miss Gordon sitting in her chair at the nursing home, gazing, gazing out over the trees. Did the trees remind her of the view she once had from her own window at Tarcoola?

Kitty pictured the lovely young woman in the photograph Andrea had found. The mysterious Mr Wolf must have been very much in love with her. And yet he betrayed her: first by marrying her when he already had a wife, then by committing suicide. That was a cruel thing to do. But even when it all came out, after he was dead, Miss Gordon still insisted that she was his wife. Why did she believe in him? He had ruined her whole life.

Kitty leaned on her elbows and closed her eyes, pressing her fingers to the lids until she could see dancing green spots in the blackness. When someone died, they left a will, and in their will they could give their money to anyone they liked, couldn't they? It didn't have to be their family – she knew that much. So even if Mr Wolf had another wife, he could still have made a will leaving everything to Miss Gordon. Why didn't he?

When Miss Gordon was upset the other day, what was it she had said? 'We won't let the wolf boy get it.' What was 'it'? The will? Maybe the wolf boy, whoever he was, wanted to destroy it so she couldn't have the house.

But no, thought Kitty. None of that made sense, because if there was a will like that she wouldn't have hidden it.

Could there be something else in the house, a sort of treasure chest? Kitty's heart beat faster. She pictured handfuls of diamond necklaces, sparkling like icicles, worth lots of money. Maybe enough to buy the house back from the other Mrs Wolf. But then, why hadn't Miss Gordon done that?

Maybe it was just the old lady's mind wandering. Mr Wolf had left her with nothing, but she didn't want to believe it.

Anyway – a thought struck Kitty – if there was a treasure chest it might not be in the house. Andrea had told her that there was not much there, and Miss Gordon herself had described the house as having gone to 'rack and ruin'. The best hiding place would be somewhere in those tunnels.

But what would happen if the house was demolished?

The picture of it flashed into Kitty's mind – the dull roar, the collapse inwards, rubble flying in slow motion, clouds of dust. All collapsing and falling into the shaft, filling it, blocking the entrance for ever and ever.

Kitty jumped up. Her mother was in the garden, as usual.

'Mum,' she called. 'Can I pick some flowers and take them to Miss Gordon?'

'That's a sweet idea, darling. Don't be long, though.'

Together they made a bouquet of daffodils, scented freesias, some daisies and a few red bottlebrushes. Kitty found some coloured paper in a drawer and carefully wrapped the flowers. Then she ran through the streets to the Sunset Home.

There was no one in the quiet entrance hall. Kitty ran lightly up the stairs. Miss Gordon was hobbling along the corridor outside her room. When she saw Kitty she pressed a finger to her lips.

'Shhhh!' she whispered. 'Don't let him see you!'

Kitty looked around in alarm. There was no one in sight.

'Who?' she asked.

'The wolf boy.' Miss Gordon leaned against the wall. Her face was white and dry, like handmade paper. Kitty took her arm.

'Look, I've brought you some flowers,' she said. She gently guided Miss Gordon back to her room.

'Oh, you're a good girl. But don't let the wolf boy see you. He tried to make me tell. Don't let him see you.'

'It's all right,' said Kitty soothingly. 'He can't see me.' She helped Miss Gordon onto the bed. The old lady was bony and fragile, and Kitty could feel her trembling.

'He'll never find it,' Miss Gordon mumbled. 'And Father's gone now. He has gone, hasn't he?'

'Oh yes, he's gone.' Did she mean her father or the wolf boy?

Kitty wondered how to broach the subject that was on her own mind. 'Did the wolf boy want your . . . your . . . the thing your husband gave you?' she ventured.

'He's always wanted it!' Miss Gordon clutched her arm, her eyes staring. 'He's at me and at me. But I won't tell!'

'Listen,' started Kitty. 'I think your treasure might be in danger. Maybe I can help—'

'Shhhh! They're listening.'

Kitty looked around nervously.

'Best not to talk about it, dear.' Miss Gordon took the bouquet from Kitty and buried her face in it. 'The lovely flowers. Mother had freesias.'

'I'll put them in a vase for you.'

Kitty went out into the corridor. A door opposite led into a sort of kitchen. She found a glass jar and filled it with water.

'Here you are!' She arranged the flowers and put them on the locker by the bed. They made the grey room almost cheerful. Miss Gordon smiled, but there were tears in her eyes.

'I don't want the wolf boy here,' she said. 'Tell them not to let him in.'

'I'll tell them.' Kitty took the frail hand in hers.

'Father knew all about it. It was up here.'

She tapped the side of her snowy head. The sparse hair stood out like feathers.

'They all looked up to him, you know. Father knew where everything was. But then the canary died, and they brought another one, and it died too. All the yellow canaries.'

She drew a daffodil from the vase and held it against her face.

'The wolf boy can't go there, you know. It's safe. It really is safe.'

'It's all right,' Kitty patted Miss Gordon's hand. 'Please don't cry.' She saw again the flying rubble, the cloud of dust that the wreckers would make. How could she tell Miss Gordon about that? Here in the nursing home, with the treetops to screen Tarcoola from view, the old lady need never know that her house was gone. But Kitty had to save the treasure!

A nurse came in and bustled over to the bed.

'Is everything all right?'

'She's upset,' admitted Kitty.

'Don't let him come back!' pleaded the old lady.

'Oh dear, she's right off the air today,' observed the nurse. 'You'd better go, love.'

'Okay.' Kitty moved reluctantly towards the door. The nurse came with her, as though to escort her off the premises. 'There's someone called the wolf boy, you see,' Kitty explained. 'I think she's scared of him.'

'Wolf boy, bogeyman,' scoffed the nurse. 'It's all in her mind.' She tapped her head meaningfully.

'Has she had a visitor?' persisted Kitty.

'Only Mr Buckingham,' said the nurse. 'You can't call him the bogeyman! He was mayor a couple of years ago. She's lucky he takes an interest in her.'

'What sort of interest?' asked Kitty.

'Pays all the extras here,' said the nurse. 'This private room, for a start. He's no relation, either – just does it out of kindness. They found her homeless, you know. Sleeping rough in some ruined house. I'm surprised they didn't put her in a mental hospital.'

'She's not mad!' said Kitty indignantly.

'Course not,' conceded the nurse. 'She's a dear old thing. Good as gold most of the time. But she's certainly out of it today!'

Kitty went slowly down the stairs and out into the street. Mr Buckingham. She would have to ask her parents if they knew who he was. She remembered a Samantha Buckingham who was at her school for a while, in Martin's year – a pretty girl, but a real snob.

There was a white car parked outside the Home with a man leaning against it, smoking. He was tall and thin, and his red hair glinted in the sun. As Kitty emerged, the man ground out his cigarette and got into the car. She heard the engine start up.

Sweetheart was also there, tied to a lamp-post.

'Hello, Sweetheart!' said Kitty, offering her hand. The dog snuffled and slobbered at it, her tail thumping. Kitty looked around to see Cec emerge from the building, spruced up in a clean shirt and a fraying tie.

'Hello, Cec!' she called.

'Hello, little lady!' Cec made his way over to her. 'Just been to see Ruby Walker. She won't last much longer, poor old soul.'

'I'll take Sweetheart.' Kitty untied the dog and took the leash in her hand. Sweetheart lumbered into motion, pointing unerringly towards home.

The white car roared off with a screech of tyres.

'Flamin' idiots!' said Cec. ''Scuse my French.'

'I've been researching local history,' said Kitty as they walked. 'Did you know that there were Japanese submarines right here in the Harbour during the war, blowing things up?'

'Well now, Win's the one to tell you about that. She hid under the table, her and her sisters. They had a fine old time of it.'

'Really? Win?'

Kitty didn't fancy asking Cec's wife about submarines or anything else. For one thing, she would have to go into the house, which was dark and smelled strongly of dog, cabbage, urine and other things she couldn't identify and didn't want to. For another thing, she had never quite got over her childish fear of Win. It was Martin's fault. He used to think it was funny to tell her that Win was an old witch who ate little children, and that was why she was so fat.

'Oh yes, Win was born in that house of ours. Me, I've only been here since we got married.'

'So you didn't know the person who committed suicide in

the Haunted House – Mr Wolf?' ventured Kitty. 'Would Win have known him?'

'Wouldn't think so. He was a Jew, you see. From – what's that place? – Checker-something. Win's Church of England.'

'And what about his wife?'

'I can remember some sort of to-do about that after the war. There was some lady who thought the first wife had been killed over there in Europe, but it turned out she'd been in America all along. Win was quite upset about it, for some reason.'

'So Win did know them?'

'She didn't say much about it. Go and ask her, if you like.'

Kitty could see she wasn't going to get any more information out of Cec. She handed over Sweetheart's leash at the corner and trudged home, lost in thought.

14

ANDREA hung around the checkouts at the supermarket for a while until her mother noticed her.

'Hey, sweetie!' Her mother looked around quickly. 'Make it fast, you know what bloody Dean'll say if he sees us.'

The woman clad in business clothes who was unloading her trolley onto the conveyor gave a little sniff of disapproval. Andrea's mother glanced at her.

'God forbid that I should do my parenting in the boss's time,' she said.

'Sorry, Mum,' said Andrea. 'I just need a bit of money. I have to go to Leichhardt, to the library.'

'Just grab my bag. It's by my feet.'

Andrea dived under the counter. Her mother watched her with one eye as she passed the woman's goods rapidly over the scanner.

'Yeah, that's right. Take ten dollars, love. The library? What's this for?'

'It's a school thing. Thanks, Mum.'

She beat a hasty retreat as the shift supervisor came out of a back room, looking askance at her mother.

The bus to Leichhardt was slow, meandering through back streets and going around in circles. She had been hoping to see something that was obviously a library, but finally, reluctantly, she realised that she would have to ask the driver.

'It's in the Italian Forum,' he said. 'I'll tell you when to get off.'

When she got there, Andrea realised that she had been to the Italian Forum before. On the way in there was a row of little shops, one of them specialising in masks. The exaggerated faces were decorated with jewels, brilliant colours, glitter and feathers, some with long, bird-like noses. She could not imagine what sort of people would buy them, and where they would wear them.

She wandered past a fountain. From one of the tables near-by came a peal of laughter and she flushed, imagining it was directed at her. The sound came from a noisy group of girls in private-school uniform, eating gelato from little silver dishes. There was one she vaguely recognised. What was her name? Vanessa? Samantha, that was it.

As Andrea stepped back out of sight she noticed a sign pointing to the library.

A grey-haired man sat at a desk. Andrea approached him confidently, flashing Kitty's library card.

'I'm looking for information from the nineteen-forties, like stuff that happened in Balmain that might have been in the papers. Could you please tell me what you've got?'

'Sorry, we don't have anything like that.'

'But the librarian at Balmain said you had all the local history.'

'We don't have anything going back that far. The local papers weren't being published then. Your best bet is to go to the State Library and look at the old *Sydney Morning Herald*s.'

'Well, do you have any information about people called Gordon? Or Wolf?' Had she really come all this way for nothing? She felt like grabbing this smug man and giving him a good shake.

'Try the internet.'

Andrea turned abruptly and nearly collided with one of the girls she had seen outside.

'Excuse me.' She brushed past the girl, who gazed curiously after her.

Andrea walked through the library and out into the plaza. People were still strolling in the late-afternoon sunshine, sitting at tables drinking coffee, chatting on mobile phones.

She saw herself going back and telling Kitty that the whole expedition had proved a waste of time, that there was no information to be had. She thought of the scanty notes that she had made on Clarissa Gordon, and the deadline Miss Tenniel had given her, coming up fast, and the phone call Miss Tenniel would make to her father, and the conversation they would have about her. She could imagine all these scenes as though she was watching a movie, and somehow it was a movie about someone else's life. It was almost as sad as Miss Gordon's life. But it didn't have to be.

She went back into the library and found the computer that was used for booking internet time. To her surprise, she only had to wait a few minutes for a terminal. While she was waiting, she scribbled a list of all the things she wanted to search for: Wolf suicide, Wolf Gordon Balmain, bombs Sydney World War II, dipthiria – could that be how you spelled it?

After a few dead ends she struck gold in an old newspaper report. 'Japanese attack Sydney Harbour!' read the headline.

The article described, in words and pictures, the night of 31 May 1942: a night of drama and chaos, when three miniature Japanese submarines, each with a two-man crew, slipped into Sydney Harbour with the intention of doing as much damage as possible before being spotted and destroyed.

It was a pretty sad story. The submarines didn't have radar or proper periscopes, so they kept having to surface and risk being seen, which of course they were. Each submarine had just two torpedoes, which they were supposed to fire at the best targets they could find. They then had a very rough plan to find their way back to their mother submarines, but nobody really expected this to work, and it didn't. None of the crew members survived – in fact one lot blew themselves up rather than be captured – and it all seemed pointless.

ANDREA printed the whole story, then moved on to her other subjects. The two hours passed in a flash, then the computer abruptly logged off. She stood, stretched and gathered her printouts and scribbled notes. The library was deserted, and outside in the plaza it was getting dark.

But when Andrea got to the bus she found a stout old woman planted in the doorway, one foot on the footpath and one foot on the bottom step, filling the entrance.

'It's supposed to be one of them kneeling buses,' she was saying.

'Not on this route, lady,' said the driver, apparently not for the first time.

'They said there'd be a kneeling bus. I can't get up them steps. I've got a bad leg.'

'Look, missus, d'you want to just wait for the next bus?'

'You said not on this route,' said the old woman sharply. 'You just want to get rid of me.'

Andrea peeped past the woman to the driver, who looked reasonably big and strong. 'Can't you just help her on?' she asked.

'Regulations,' he shrugged. 'Health and safety. If I do me back or something, I wouldn't be able to claim.'

'Oh, for heaven's sake.' Andrea considered pushing, but she didn't fancy getting her hands under that bulging bottom. Instead, she squeezed past and onto the bus. Shoving her folder of papers under her arm, she swung her schoolbag onto her back, turned and took a firm grip on the woman's arm. With a tremendous heave, she managed to get the woman up the steps and onto the bus, where they collapsed together onto the front seats as the vehicle lurched into motion.

Andrea's papers scattered over the floor.

Only then did Andrea realise she'd been holding on to Cec's wife, Win. Win was usually parked in front of the TV in their dark little house, glued to the sports program.

'Thank you dear, thank you so much!' Win wheezed as Andrea scrambled around, collecting her papers. 'What a good girl you are. You're that little girl from Christina Street, aren't you? Very helpful little girl. I always say that kids these days . . . Well! Will you look at that!'

She had picked up the printout about the submarines and was reading it with fascination, her mouth hanging open.

'Well, well, well,' she said. 'What a night that was!'

'Were you around when it happened?' asked Andrea.

'Ha! We were all under the table, my sisters and me. Boom! We found out later they were right over the other side, but it sounded much closer. Kept on going for hours. We were that scared!' She sighed. 'Poor little Clarissa. That was the night Josef Woolf . . . you know.'

'What?'

'Oh, you're just a kid,' Win patted Andrea's shoulder soothingly. 'Shouldn't talk about such things.'

'No, it's all right.' Andrea was struggling to stay calm, to be nice. Kitty, Kitty, I need you now, she was thinking. She touched the old woman's squishy knee.

'Please tell me what happened.'

'Well – I didn't know meself until much later. I was only a little thing at the time. It was Vi told me eventually.'

'Vi?'

'She was the oldest. She's passed on now. There were five of us. All girls. Poor old Dad. People used to say it was because of the soap factory.'

'So what did Vi tell you? About Mr Wolf?'

'Yes. Woolf with two Os, you know. He was from one of those funny European countries. They're all different now.'

'And what happened to him?'

'Seems he was that scared with all the noise, he must've thought the Japs were coming for sure. Who knows what he thought. Anyway, poor chap shot himself.' She shuddered, sending all her chins trembling. 'Don't know how Clarissa slept through it, but she musta done. Didn't find him till the next morning.'

'Oh!' Andrea was lost for words. She knew that Miss Gordon hadn't slept through it. She would have been down in the bomb shelter, and he must have gone up to the house to kill himself. Andrea imagined the scene as Miss Gordon crept upstairs in the morning, searching room by room for her beloved Mr Woolf.

'Ah, that was all a long time ago.' Win patted her hand. 'I shouldn't have told you.'

She settled back and seemed to fall into a doze. Andrea took out one of her printouts and scribbled notes on the back, looking up with a start as Win started painfully hauling herself to her feet.

'This your stop too, dear?'

'No. Ummm . . . Yeah, sure.'

The bus driver looked the other way while the old lady struggled to get out. Andrea couldn't stand it, especially when Win had been so unexpectedly helpful. She jumped down from the bus and held Win's hands as the old lady tentatively put first one foot then another onto terra firma.

It didn't end there. Andrea was about to dart away but Win, clearly tired and a little shaky, took her arm, so there was nothing for it but to set off at a snail's pace for the old lady's house, mercifully not too far away.

'Those doctors,' Win muttered. 'Sending me all the way to Leichhardt for me leg. They don't know what it does to a poor old woman. And I've still got to get Cec his tea, and something for Sweetheart. I've got a nice bit of casserole left. That'll do him. Or would she like it? I'll make a steak-and-kidney pie tomorrow. Clarissa liked that.'

Suddenly Andrea tuned in. 'You cooked for Clarissa?'

Win stopped dead. 'Now I didn't say that, did I?'

They started walking again.

'I've met Clarissa,' said Andrea. 'My friend goes to see her, and sometimes I go too. She's a really sweet old lady.'

'My sister Vi loved her,' said Win. 'Vi was what they called a Tarcoola girl. Used to work at Josef Woolf's house. There's none of them left now.' She sighed. 'I didn't really know Clarissa meself, but I was always happy to take the bits and pieces to her. I did it for Vi, really, and the other Tarcoola girls.'

'But when was this? You said you were only little when Mr Woolf died.'

'That's right. The other Mrs Woolf kicked Clarissa out after the war, and she disappeared for a while. Went off housekeeping somewhere, the girls thought. We started bringing her the food, sort of on the quiet, when she came back.'

'How long did she stay in the house?'

'Oh, years, on and off. Only the Tarcoola girls knew she was there. They looked after her. She got caught eventually and they put her in the Home.'

They were at Win's gate by now. Win pulled Andrea close.

'You won't mention this to Cec, will you?' she whispered. 'He's funny about some things. Trespassing, and that. He never did know she was there.'

'That's fine,' Andrea gave her a little hug. 'And thank you so much for telling me.'

The old lady hobbled up the path to her house. As soon as her key scraped in the lock, a frantic barking began inside. Andrea turned and ran.

15

T H E alarm chirped at six o'clock on Friday morning. Andrea grabbed the clock and turned the alarm off before it could sound again. Across the room Celeste cursed and pulled the bedclothes over her head.

Andrea picked up her books and tiptoed to the kitchen. The table was cluttered with dirty plates, newspapers and coffee cups. She pushed them to one side, making a space in which to work. Holding her nose, she picked up the brimming ashtray and put it outside the back door.

The draft was finished. Andrea laid out some sheets of paper, took the new black pen she had bought, and began to write in her clear, round running-writing. As she started each new page she examined her stock of illustrations – the copy of Miss Gordon's photograph, the printouts from the library, the photos she had taken of the house and the bomb shelter – and worked out how to incorporate each one into the layout.

Andrea wrote steadily on while the pink light creeping through the blinds gradually intensified to gold. She finished with a flourish and then read the whole thing through to herself.

THE GHOST THAT WASN'T
a Historical Biography by Andrea McKinley-Brown

*Clarissa Gordon was born on the 2nd of January 1919
in a small house in Christina Street, Balmain. She was
not born in a hospital because her parents were poor.
The house where she was born is renovated now (see
photo) but it still only has two bedrooms, so it must have
been very small then, and Clarissa's mother had nine
children, she really had more than nine children, but some
of them died when they were babies. A lot of babies died
in those days especially in poor families like the Gordons.
One died from diphtheria that babies don't get these days
because they are all immunised. One died of Spanish Flu
in the 1918 pandemic that spread to nearly every part
of the world (see Wikipedia extract).*

*Mr Gordon used to work in a coal mine, but they
closed the pit after a while and then he worked on the
wharves but there was precious little to be had there
when the depression started. Mr Gordon couldn't go
on the wallaby because he had so many children and
Mrs Gordon couldn't work either with so many children
so Clarissa had to go out to work and she went into
Service she was probably about twelve. Being in Service
she was a servant in a big house where she had to get up
before dawn and work all day.*

When Clarissa grew up she was very beautiful
(see photo). She met a rich man called Mr Woolf who
fell madly in love with her. Mr Woolf had just come
from Czechoslovakia (now the Czech Republic) because
there was the Second World War in Europe and he was
scared. He bought a big house in Birchgrove called
Tarcoola (see photo) and a factory next to it and he asked
Clarissa to marry him and gave her lots of presents. Little
did she know he was already married. They had a big
wedding and went to the Great Barrier Reef for their
honeymoon. Clarissa was very happy being the mistress
of Tarcoola and being Mrs Woolf. They lived well and
had parties, but Mr Woolf was still worried about the
war. He built an air-raid shelter under his house he was
so scared. He put in gas masks (see photo) and food and
books in German.

On the 31st of May, 1942, three Japanese submarines
invaded Sydney Harbour (see newspaper report).
They torpedoed an old ferry called the Kuttabul and
killed nineteen sailors (see photo). The water police
chased them around the Harbour and finally blew one of
them out of the water. All the people who lived near the
harbour could hear the explosions and see the searchlights.
The noise was so loud it shook their houses and broke
their windows. Some people were very scared and hid
under the table. Mr Woolf got extremely upset thinking

*the Japanese invasion was starting and it was just as bad
as Europe which he had left to get away from the war so
he took his wife down to their bomb shelter and told
her to stay there. But then he got more and more depressed
and finally he went up to the house and committed
suicide. He didn't leave a note and didn't tell his wife
he was going to do it. He made her stay in the shelter
and she didn't know what had happened to him until
the next day.*

*Clarissa was very upset and in a State of Shock,
but she carried on living in the house and looking after
everything. But a few years later Mr Woolf's first wife
turned up she had been in America and she came back
and said the house and the factory belonged to her. This
was true because if a man doesn't make a will his wife
gets everything (see photocopy from Year 11 Legal Studies
textbook). Mr Woolf should of made a will because he
knew Clarissa wasn't his real wife, or he should of given
Clarissa some money of her own, but he didn't get round
to it so she had a really bad time and after living the life
of a rich lady and the mistress of Tarcoola now she was
poor again.*

*After the real Mrs Woolf came back and took
everything, Clarissa was too ashamed to go back to her
family, because people in those days thought bigamy was
a big disgrace even though it wasn't her fault. So she*

*just disappeared she probably went and worked as a
housekeeper somewhere far away. The real Mrs Woolf
went back to America, nobody came to live in Tarcoola
and the house got more and more wrecked. Years later,
in the 1990s, they closed the factory.*

*BUT nobody knew that after many years away
Clarissa came back and lived secretly in the house.
She used to spend a lot of time looking out the window
and daydreaming about the good times she used to have.
Sometimes children saw her there and she looked scary
because her face was all wrinkled by now and her beauty
gone and naturally they thought she was a ghost and
everybody called Tarcoola the Haunted House. The old
ladies in the area who had been the servants at Tarcoola
called Tarcoola girls used to bring her food (sorry I cannot
disclose my source).*

*When Clarissa couldn't hide any more they put her
in the Sunset Home (see photo), and she is still living
there today.*

*Tarcoola is still empty and wrecked and some people
still think it's haunted and if nobody stops them the
developers will pull it down and build town houses there
even though the house is very old and has Historical
Significance (see newspaper report).*

THE END

When Andrea had finished the last page, she took the folder she had found under Celeste's bed, wiped the grubby plastic with a damp kitchen sponge, and dried it with a clean tea towel. Then she placed her work carefully inside and packed it into her bag.

A hacking cough announced the arrival of her mother, who groped her way blearily into the kitchen and, apparently from memory, filled the kettle and plugged it in.

'You're up early, love. Feeling all right?'

'Sure,' said Andrea. 'The garbos woke me, banging the bins, and I couldn't get back to sleep.'

'Well, get yourself some breakfast.' Her mother lit up a cigarette. 'Where the hell's that ashtray gone?'

HISTORY was the last period of the day. Miss Tenniel arrived armed to the teeth with a class set of textbooks and a stack of printouts, all of which she distributed with the help of some of the keener students. Andrea stuck out her tongue at Martin as he delivered a printout to her desk.

'Watch out!' he hissed. 'You'll get detention if you're not careful.'

Andrea grinned and picked up her sheet. 'Aw, Miss!' she exclaimed loudly. 'Fifteen questions. It's Friday afternoon!'

'That's why I'm giving you such easy work,' said Miss Tenniel calmly. 'Now class, I expect you to finish at least the first ten questions this period.'

At the end of the lesson Andrea bounded out of the room with the front-runners, as usual. Halfway down the corridor she stopped and slapped her forehead dramatically.

'Forgot my pen!' she announced, heading back to the classroom.

Miss Tenniel was still packing up her papers. Andrea sidled up and placed her assignment on the desk. She turned to flee.

'Wait a minute, Andrea.' Miss Tenniel picked up the folder and started turning pages. 'This looks very interesting!' She read for a while. Andrea shuffled her feet.

'Is this all your own work, Andrea?'

Andrea flushed. 'I don't copy, Miss.'

'Of course not! I didn't mean that. But you seem to have done a lot of work. Where did you get these photos?'

'I took some, and the old lady gave me that one.'

Miss Tenniel flicked though some more pages. 'Well, Andrea, you've set yourself quite a standard here!' She smiled. 'Do you think you could do more of this kind of work?'

'I dunno,' muttered Andrea. 'I might.'

'You might. Well, we'll see how it goes.' Miss Tenniel packed the assignment into her satchel. 'And if you have any problems, Andrea, with the work, or . . . or at home, you can always come to me, you know.'

'All right. Thanks, Miss.'

Andrea hurried along the deserted corridor and out into the school grounds. Only a few stragglers were left, and there was no one she knew in the yard. She took a short cut across the soccer field and went out the side gate, which the caretaker was about to lock.

As she started walking briskly along the footpath she heard a car engine purr into life. She was wondering what Miss Tenniel would think of the bit about the submarines. And should she have put in that stuff about the will?

She was about to cross a side street when a white car nosed in front of her and stopped, blocking her way. A man got out of the passenger seat. He was short and stocky, with dark hair growing low on his forehead.

'Hullo, love.' He had a flat New Zealand accent. 'Wanna earn some money?'

Andrea glanced in disbelief at the fifty-dollar note he was holding in front of her face.

'Excuse me,' she said stiffly, edging to one side. The footpath was narrow, and there was not enough room to pass the man without getting uncomfortably close to him.

'Come on, get in.' His tone was sharper now. 'We only wanna talk to you.'

Andrea glanced into the car. The windows were tinted and the red-haired man at the wheel kept his face turned away, but there was something definitely menacing about his upper arm, heavily muscled and wreathed in tattoos.

The New Zealander was still blocking her way, waiting for an answer. There was no one else in the street. Andrea made up her mind what to do.

'Let me past!' she said clearly, but at the same time she took a few steps backwards and tightened her grip on her schoolbag. The man grinned and spread his arms wide, and she spun and ran back the way she had come.

Andrea was a good runner, and she didn't expect much trouble from the short-legged New Zealander, but the other man was more of a worry. If he decided to get out of the car and chase her she might be in trouble. However, to her relief, she heard the engine start up, and much revving as he tried to turn the car in the narrow street. This would buy her some time.

She ran hard, her bag bumping uncomfortably against her side. She could hear pounding footsteps behind her, getting closer.

Just past the school there was a dunny path, one of a network of narrow back lanes behind the terrace houses. This one led through several turns to other lanes, and eventually came out in another street. Even if she didn't manage to lose the New Zealander, Andrea was confident that she could use that route to get away from the car.

Andrea ducked into the dunny path at the last possible minute. She heard the New Zealander thunder past, and the sudden silence as he stopped, trying to take in what had happened. Then she was away, flying down the narrow lane, twisting round the bends.

She shot out into the next street and glanced quickly both ways. She groaned. The white car was crawling across the intersection to her right. Luckily it was a fair distance away –

she was much closer to the other corner. The New Zealander was panting behind her, so she had no choice. She raced across the road, her breath rasping painfully now, and round the corner to the left. The blocks in this street were short, and she had a good chance of getting into the next street before they could see which way she had gone.

Andrea was concentrating so hard on her escape that she had almost reached the next corner before things fell into place in her mind. David lived in this street.

There it was, a two-storey terrace house with a bare-branched frangipani tree at the front. She ran up the path and pounded on the door. She could hear the car turning into the street. Any minute now it would come past, and they would see her.

David himself answered the door. He stared at Andrea.

'Quick. Someone's after me.' She pushed past him. 'Come on, shut the door.'

He shut it. Andrea pressed herself against the wall of the hallway, panting. David found his voice.

'Who's after you?'

'How would I know? Two men.' Andrea was out of breath. 'I can't go out there.'

She looked along the hallway. Through one door the dining room was visible, with a glowing polished table and richly patterned rugs. At the end she could glimpse a living room, late afternoon sunlight slanting onto colourful cushions and piles of books.

'Come up.'

She followed him up the stairs. David removed some clothes from an armchair for her, then sat down on a straight-backed chair in front of a computer. Andrea sidled over to the window and peeped through the curtains, but all she could see was the brick wall of the house next door.

'What happened?' persisted David.

'They were scary.' She came back and flopped into the armchair. 'There was a car. They tried to get me to go with them. One of them got out and chased me. I didn't want them to find out where I live.'

'Did they see you come in here?'

'Maybe. I was running. I don't think they came around the corner in time.'

David went into the front room and she could see him peering through the slatted blinds. He returned to Andrea.

'What sort of car?'

'Just a white car. Fairly big. Just a car.'

'There are two white cars parked out there. Can't see if there's anyone in them. And a white car sort of cruised past while I was looking.'

'Maybe that was them, looking for me.'

'Hell, Andrea, every second car is white.'

'Don't you believe me?' she challenged. 'Do you want me to go?'

'Course not. Maybe we should ring the police.'

'Police?' Andrea was scornful. 'They won't do anything.'

'But they tried to kidnap you. They're dangerous.'

'There are lots of men like that out there,' Andrea told him. 'They tried to pick up my sister once, but the police didn't believe her. You just have to be really careful.'

'Oh.' David sounded a bit shocked. 'You'd better stay here, then. Wait until it's safe.' He turned to his computer.

Andrea stared at her feet for a while, brooding. Then she watched David as he rapidly dragged things around the screen.

'What are you doing?'

'I'm making this city, see? I have to build roads, and bridges, and factories for the people to work in. But I can't let it get too polluted.'

'How long have you been at it?'

'About fifty years,' he answered, not looking up as he zoomed in on some tiny, unidentifiable object.

Andrea burst out laughing. David looked bewildered, then he laughed too.

'Sorry. I mean it's fifty years in the game. I started yesterday after school, and I got up early to play some more. I was up at six o'clock this morning.'

'Were you? So was I. I had an assignment to finish. And you'd better not say anything,' she added quickly, seeing the beginnings of an incredulous smile.

David tapped some keys. Andrea looked around the room. A bed was faintly discernible under some clothes in a corner.

'Funny,' she mused. 'I always thought your room would be really tidy.'

'Well, I bet yours is messy.'

'It is not. Not my half, anyway. It's extremely well-organised. All six square metres of it.'

They both stared at the screen.

'How come you have the computer in your room?' she asked idly.

'Well . . . It's my computer.'

'Oh, right.'

Andrea began to wander around the room, picking things up and putting them down. She stopped in front on a photograph of David and Martin, clowning in ski gear, a snow-covered mountain in the background.

'When was this?'

'Last year. Mr Mac took the whole class to the snow in third term. Martin went from beginners to advanced in one week, and I broke my leg.'

'I really missed Martin when they put me in a different class in Year Six. I used to hang out with him all the time.'

'Yeah, I miss him now,' said David. 'It kind of sucks, going to different high schools.'

'It kind of sucks going to my high school,' said Andrea.

David tapped some keys.

'It must be good, though, being with Marty,' he said.

'I hardly ever see him.'

'Oh.' He didn't look up. 'I thought he was – kind of – your boyfriend?'

'I don't know why people say that.'

'What, isn't he?'

'Not that I know of. He's never asked me.'

'Does he have to ask you?'

'Course he does.' Why didn't boys understand these things? 'If he reckons we're going out, he has to ask me.'

David stopped typing. 'So then you'll be going out with him?'

'Depends. I'd have to say yes.'

'And what if someone else asks you?'

Now he was teasing her. She jumped up. 'What's the time?'

David looked at his watch. 'Nearly four. I've got to turn on the oven.'

'Why?'

'It's my turn to put the dinner on tonight. It's one of my mum's slow-cooked gourmet things.'

'I do spaghetti,' said Andrea. 'That's my specialty. You'd lo-o-ove my spaghetti.'

'I bet I'd like it more than my mum's gourmet stuff.' He grinned at her.

'Well – I'd better go.' She picked up her bag.

'Do you think it's safe now?' asked David.

'I guess so. Maybe . . . is there a back lane?'

'Yeah. Come on, I'll show you.'

They clattered downstairs into the tidy kitchen.

'Wow,' said Andrea. 'Do your parents use all these gadgets?'

'Sure,' said David, looking around. 'My grandfather, too. They're always having dinner parties and stuff, even though my dad works, like, eighty hours a week.'

He led her through the narrow garden. A furry white cat emerged from the bushes and wound itself around Andrea's ankles.

'He likes you,' said David. 'He usually hisses at visitors.'

'Well, thanks,' said Andrea, bending down to scratch behind the cat's ears. 'I mean – for letting me come in.'

'Will you be okay now? Should I come with you?'

'No, I know a back way from here. They'll never find me.'

David hesitated. He looked as though he was about to say something else, but whatever it was, the moment passed.

'See you, then.' He held open the gate and Andrea slipped out into the gathering shadows.

16

MARTIN skidded in the mud and went down on one knee. As he leapt to his feet the ball flew out of the pack towards him. 'Marty! It's yours!' He twisted around and kicked in one action. It was an awkward angle and he had to use his left foot, but the ball flew straight and true, and the goalie jumped the wrong way. Cheers erupted around the ground. Martin ran over and punched the boundary marker like his hero Tim Cahill. Team-mates raced up to clap him on the back.

A few minutes later, the final whistle blew. Martin was wet, muddy and sore from various encounters with the slippery ground, but the coach shook his hand, saying 'Well done, mate,' and his father was grinning proudly on the sidelines.

Martin stripped off his soccer jersey and threw it on the pile, then sauntered over to his father's car to get his jumper. Someone was leaning against a sleek black Mercedes, watching him. Martin caught her eye, then quickly looked away. Samantha Buckingham's long blonde hair was like spun gold, her expensive clothes always immaculate. She had been in his class at primary school for a while, but left after Year Four to start at a private school a few suburbs away, and he rarely saw her these days. Usually she looked straight through him.

'Hi, Martin!' She had come very close. The jumper was halfway over his head, and he was aware of his sweaty body.

'Great game,' Samantha went on.

'Yeah, pretty good.' Martin had got his head free now. 'Wasn't enough to get us into the finals, though.'

'Better luck next year.' Samantha's voice was smooth, almost caressing. Martin was torn between wishing she would go away before he made a fool of himself, and wanting to make her stay. He searched for something to say.

'You interested in soccer?'

'Sure.' She smiled winningly. 'My dad's just talking to the coach.' She inclined her head. Martin saw a balding man in a suit talking to Ted Wallace. A plump fair boy hovered next to them, fiddling with an iPhone.

'Oliver wants to play in the under twelves next year,' Samantha explained. 'He didn't get selected this season, so my dad's making a donation to the club.'

'Oh.' Martin couldn't see the logic, but it didn't matter. A number of his team-mates were looking his way. Just a few months ago Martin would have died of embarrassment at being seen talking to a girl, but right now he was feeling good, having scored the team's only goal for the match, and Samantha was very pretty.

'How's school?' asked Samantha.

'Oh – all right. I'm doing Chinese.' This always impressed his parents' friends.

'Really? We do French, Latin and Japanese.' Samantha

examined her fingernails, which were painted pale pink. 'We've got our first formal at the end of this term.'

'Yeah?' What was a formal? Martin wondered. Some sort of exam?

'I'm having a dress made. There was nothing but rubbish in the shops.'

'Oh! Cool.'

'The trouble is' – she frowned a little – 'I need a partner. I can't take my brother.' She shot a contemptuous glance at the offending Oliver, who was trying out different ringtones while his father earbashed Ted. 'He's too short.'

Samantha herself was on the small side, Martin reflected. She came about up to his eyebrows.

'So would you be interested?' Samantha went on.

'Huh?'

'You don't have to,' she added hastily. To Martin's amazement her face had turned a delicate pink. Was the princess actually blushing?

'Oh! No, I'd . . . But I've never been to . . . that sort of thing.'

'You'd have to wear a suit. Maybe you could hire one,' she added helpfully.

'Well, um . . . I'll find out. I could ask my parents.'

'Fabulous.' She gave him a dazzling smile. 'It's not for about three weeks. Wanna give me your number?'

She was making the universal phone sign with finger and thumb. Martin groaned inwardly.

'Oh, I'm . . . uh . . . between phones at the moment.'

'Don't worry, I'll find you on Facebook. Send you the details.' She reached up and gave him a quick kiss on the cheek.

'Sure.' Still dazzled, Martin watched her walk away.

'That Harold Buckingham!' snorted Martin's father in the car going home. 'He thinks he can buy anything he wants.'

'They're really rich, aren't they?' said Martin.

'Oh, sure. But all he thinks about is making more money. And spoiling his kids.' Martin's father gave him a shrewd look. 'Did I see you chatting up his daughter?'

'No! I mean – she was chatting me up.'

His father chuckled. 'You kids get it easy. In my day the boys had to do all the work.'

Martin decided not to mention Samantha's invitation. He wanted some time to think about it. The thought of wearing a suit and doing all those dances the teachers had made them learn in Year Six made him quail. But then, if news got around that he was escorting Samantha Buckingham, that of all the boys around she had chosen him . . . It was amazing what scoring a goal in soccer could bring you!

CLEANED up, fed and still feeling good, Martin jogged through the newly washed back streets to David's house. The sun had struggled through the last of the clouds, and dogs were out sniffing the footpaths.

David was engrossed in his computer screen.

'Eureka!' he said. 'Hi.'

'What's happening?' Martin peered over his shoulder.

'My city's now entering the year 2075, and I've doubled the population over the last ten years. Hong and Michael only got to 2050, then they had a nuclear plant explosion and got wiped out. I told them they shouldn't mine uranium!' David punched the keys gleefully. 'Sucked in, Hong!'

'Sounds good,' said Martin, flopping down on the bed. 'I bring you a mini Mars Bar, o lord of the city.' He dug it out of his pocket.

'I graciously accept.' David turned around in his chair and put a hand out. 'How was soccer?'

'Not too bad. I got a goal.'

'Only one?'

'Well, you know how it is. I didn't want to take too much glory on myself.' Martin watched David eat the Mars Bar, his eyes wandering occasionally back to the screen. 'Are you going to keep playing that, or what?'

'Nah, I'll save it.' David's fingers flew over the keys. 'Did Andrea tell you about the bomb shelter? D'you want to have a look?'

'Sure.' Martin jumped to his feet. 'Kitty's coming too. She said she'd meet us in the garden.'

'Right.' David zipped through a sequence of coloured screens until the last one was finally sucked into oblivion. He turned to Martin.

'There's a big meeting in the Town Hall on Monday night, about the development. I might go.'

'You said they were really boring!'

'Well, they are. But they're going to wreck the Haunted House. I'd like to find out what people are doing to stop it. Do you want to come?'

'I just might have a lot of homework that night.'

'Whatever.'

When they reached Tarcoola, Kitty and Andrea were waiting impatiently beside the lily pond.

'We've eaten all the—' started Kitty, but Martin had wrestled her to the ground and got her backpack open before she could manage another word, and they were soon demolishing chocolate-chip muffins.

Martin brushed the crumbs off his hands and reached into his own backpack.

'Wanna see my map?' He untied the red ribbon and unrolled it a little shyly.

'Hey, Martin, that's really beautiful!' Andrea was obviously surprised.

He had certainly spent a lot of time on it, working with watercolour paints and ink, using subtle colour distinctions to show the areas they had explored and the areas that were still unknown. He had put in faint trails showing where he thought some of the tunnels might lead, and several 'Here be monsters' images.

'So you think there are tunnels under our feet right now?' mused David.

'Makes sense, don't you think? Remember the tunnel we couldn't get through, the first day, when we ended up under the house? It was heading this way.'

'But you've suggested a whole network,' said Kitty, frowning at the map.

'Yeah, well, there's a mixture of natural tunnels and man-made tunnels. I'm sort of wondering if some of them join up.' Martin mentally hugged himself as he considered the map-making possibilities.

'Should we explore the house first?' said Kitty. 'It might have sliding panels and hidden staircases and all that kind of stuff.'

'I don't think so,' said Andrea. 'I had a good look round the other day, and it's pretty bare.'

'Yeah, I really want to get back into those tunnels,' said Martin. 'I've just got a feeling there should be a nice exit somewhere here in the garden, through a maze or something.'

'Not too many mazes in this garden,' observed David.

'Still . . . My map is telling me there's something missing. I say we check out that tunnel with the fallen rocks.'

'But this is silly,' said Kitty impatiently. 'Andrea and I didn't come here to draw a map and run around finding secret exits. We've got to find Miss Gordon's thing, her special present.'

'Huh?' said Martin.

'Didn't we decide that some of what Miss Gordon says—' Andrea started.

'Forget all that,' interrupted David, 'I say we should—'

'Stop!' cried Kitty. 'You're not listening! There's something hidden in there, and it's really, really important!'

There was a brief silence.

'What sort of something?' asked David.

'Well, maybe . . . like . . . some kind of treasure?'

'Kitty, I don't really think . . .'

'Listen, every time I've talked to Clarissa – Miss Gordon – she's been all worried about something that Mr Woolf gave her, this present thing. No, listen!' This was to Martin, who was packing his map away, eager to be off. 'She's been keeping it hidden all this time. If they demolish the house we won't be able to find it. It'll be lost for ever!'

'But you don't even know what it is, Kitty,' said Andrea.

'No, but I'm sure it's something really, really valuable. And if we find it for her she won't be poor and maybe . . . maybe she could buy the house back? It could be, like, a fabulous diamond necklace . . . or . . . or something?'

'Yeah, sure,' began Martin, but Andrea silenced him with a look.

'And anyway,' said Kitty. 'There's this really scary man she calls the wolf boy and he wants it too. So it's not just her.' She was close to tears.

'Okay,' said David patiently. 'Well, we want to explore anyway, so let's just keep a look out for it. How about that? There's not much else we can do, because we don't know what it is, and we don't know where it is.'

'All right,' muttered Kitty.

'And we might as well go with Martin's idea, too,' David went on. 'It would be great to find another exit so we can get into the tunnels without the risk of getting caught in the house.'

Andrea put a supportive arm around Kitty as they made their way to the house. She led the way to the glass doors at the side of the house, which were still unlocked, and into the cellar. They went down the ladder, carefully closing the trap-door behind them.

'So let's see this place with the gas masks and everything,' said Kitty.

They crowded into the bomb shelter. Kitty insisted on examining everything, while Martin searched for undiscovered doorways. David and Andrea hovered impatiently around the exit. Finally Martin was satisfied.

'Okay, no way out here. Let's go!'

In the main shaft, Martin checked his map for accuracy.

'Right,' he said. 'Four entrances. South is the bomb shelter, which we've just come out of. West is the door we originally came in through, with the twisty passage leading to the Dough-nut. East is the other door with the missing key, and north is the big tunnel where the cathedral is, and David's Leap.'

'Oh, is that marked on the map?' asked David, looking pleased. 'I didn't notice.'

Andrea gave a little sniff.

'Or maybe it could be Andrea's Chasm?' David offered.

'Andrea's Agony, more like,' she said, sticking out a wiry leg in torn-off denim. The scratches were scabbed over, but the bruises had reached a spectacular multi-coloured stage.

'Come on, let's get going,' said Martin. This time he had equipped himself with a working torch. He switched it on and plunged through the unlocked door into the west tunnel. At the fork in the tunnel they had found on the first day, he turned left, confident of finding the rock-fall that had stopped them from going any further.

'Martin! Where are you?' He could hear Kitty's voice, wavering in the sour-smelling darkness.

'Where do you think?' he called back impatiently, pulling at the rocks that blocked his way.

Within a few seconds the others joined him. David shone his torch beam around the walls.

'If we just take them from the top, maybe we can go over?' he suggested.

'Give it a go,' grunted Martin.

They all worked quickly, moving and stacking the rocks until there was a space big enough to crawl through. On the other side, the tunnel stretched on into blackness.

'Yes!' said Martin, exchanging a high-five with David.

For what seemed like hours they explored, going up one dead-end tunnel after another, lowering themselves through holes in the floor, clambering up through holes in the ceiling, scrambling out backwards when there wasn't room to turn around. Martin showed them the right marks to make on the tunnel walls at every intersection, while he sketched a new section of the map.

Kitty had had enough after ten minutes, and occupied herself by looking behind rocks and in small fissures in the walls, and any other likely hiding places for treasure.

Then, miraculously, Martin found what he was looking for: a tunnel leading upwards with steps hewn into the rock.

'See,' he said triumphantly, as his torch beam caressed the stone edges. 'There's a reason for this.'

However, at the top of the steps he was disappointed to find a short ladder with steel rungs, leading nowhere. There was no trapdoor, just earth, roots and a jumble of rocks. He looked down at the others in disgust.

'Well, this isn't right,' he said. 'It doesn't make sense at all.'

'There must have been an exit once,' said David. 'Something's collapsed and the stones have filled the hole, then dirt and stuff must have kind of piled up on top.'

'Well, let's dig it out,' said Andrea. 'I saw some tools in the bomb shelter. What's the quickest way back, Marty?'

'Wait,' said David. 'We can't do it from below. If we start hacking at that soil the rocks'll just fall on our heads. We've got to figure out where the entrance is up top and dig down.'

'Okaaaaayyyy.' Martin sat down and studied his map. The others looked at him expectantly.

'What are you looking at me for?'

'Well,' said Andrea. 'What sort of a mapmaker are you?'

'Well, come on. It'd be different if I had a GPS or something.'

'I've got a GPS on my phone!' David pulled it out. They all crowded around.

'I've got a good signal. We must be close to the surface. Come on, come on. Stop jiggling, Kitty. I can't see it properly. Ah, here it comes . . . Hmmm. It says we're in Ultimo.'

They sat down at the foot of the ladder, dejected. Kitty handed around some apples.

'The next model's better, apparently,' said David. 'Much more accurate.'

'That's good to know,' said Andrea drily.

'We could use Andrea's and David's phones, though,' said Kitty. 'See, we could have one down here, and one up top. And one lot of us could make a loud noise, and the others could call on the phone when they hear it, and when it gets louder, and so on.'

'Hey, that's not a bad idea!' Martin brightened immediately.

'You'd have to call me,' Andrea said. They all chorused with her: 'I've got no credit.'

She took David's phone. 'You wouldn't have my number,' she said, a little shyly. 'I'll put it in your contacts.'

'It'd have to be a pretty loud noise, though,' Martin went on. 'What have we got to make a noise with?'

'Maybe we could shout?' offered Andrea.

'Maybe,' said David doubtfully, taking his phone back. 'It'd be good if we had a whistle or something. Marty, doesn't your dad do some umpiring? Wouldn't there be a whistle at your place?'

'What, you want me to go all the way home and look for a whistle? Why do I have to—'

Andrea's phone suddenly shrilled.

'Sorry,' said David. 'I hit the call button.'

'Whoa, Andrea,' cried Martin, putting his hands over his ears. 'Could you make it a bit louder?'

The others all started laughing as Andrea shut the phone off, and he looked at them in bewilderment. 'What? What did I say?'

Once they had worked out the details of the plan, the boys made their way back, picking up a mattock and shovel from the bomb shelter on the way. Martin had a rough idea of the general direction, and they agreed that they were looking for a spot in the garden at the side, rather than the front of the house. There would have to be trees, to account for the roots they had seen, and possibly some kind of stone structure.

The girls were left in semi-darkness, with just Martin's torch. Andrea had suggested that they also get some spades, but David was adamantly against it.

'Bad idea!' he had said. 'Remember what we said before? You don't want to be anywhere near the ladder when we start shifting that dirt.'

When they made the first phone call to Andrea, Martin could hear Kitty in the background plaintively asking: 'Is that it? Have they found it?'

'We're close,' he told Andrea. 'David thought he could hear something when your phone started ringing.'

'Where are you?'

'Near a rose garden.'

'Any ruined buildings?'

'No, nothing.'

'Hey, what about the naked lady?' said Andrea. 'That was all broken around the bottom. Go and have a look.'

'What are you talking about?'

'David knows.'

David grinned and led Martin through the roses to a statue on a broken base. The white lady gazed modestly downwards. They searched around her feet, but there was nothing but dead grass and cracked earth. David called Andrea again.

'Good guess!' he said. 'We definitely heard your phone this time. Yeah. Yeah. No, we're sort of at the side. There's nothing here.'

He looked up at Martin.

'She says we should try around the back. Makes sense.'

There was a narrow space between the statue and the trees. The base was badly damaged on one corner. They pulled a couple of large stones away and called Andrea again.

This time they heard the phone ringing loud and clear, and they exchanged a high-five, whooping with glee. Andrea picked up immediately.

'Hey, we heard you yelling!' she said. 'Better start digging!'

The two boys worked hard and as carefully as they could,

but as soon as a gap appeared there was a yelp from below.

'Stand back!' called David.

'Sorry,' came Andrea's voice. 'I see what you mean.'

Eventually the hole was big enough and Martin lowered himself down.

'Come on!' he called to the girls waiting below.

Andrea and Kitty climbed up and emerged into the sunlight. The entrance was well hidden in a tangle of undergrowth, and they arranged the broken stones to look undisturbed, but so they could get in again without too much effort.

'Brilliant!' Martin kept saying. 'Brilliant!'

Kitty gave him half a banana and he scoffed it down.

'This is great,' he said, looking around. 'We can come and go from the lane. If there are security guys in the house they won't see us.'

'So how will all this appear on your map?' asked Andrea.

'Dunno. I'll have to think up a sort of puzzle for this entrance. You know, kind of "Speak friend and enter". Have to give it some thought. What food have you got left, Kitty?'

To his dismay, Kitty's backpack was empty.

'We have to go, anyway,' said Kitty. 'We can come back tomorrow.'

'Okay.' David picked up the mattock and shovel. 'Let's leave the torches in the bomb shelter with the tools. My folks have got people coming to lunch tomorrow, and they're kind of expecting me to be there. So Marty, can you come round at about two-ish with a really complicated maths problem?

As in, a whole assignment?'

'I reckon I could do that. Earlier if you like.'

'No, I want a chance to grab something to eat before you tear me away.'

'David,' asked Kitty, 'will Moshe be making one of those cakes?'

'A kugelhopf? You can bet your life on it.'

'Any chance you can smuggle some out?'

'I'll give it a go. We could be lucky.'

They separated, feeling they had done a good afternoon's work.

Kitty was quiet on the way home. Still, thought Martin, no use worrying about her. The only thing that would make her happy was finding her so-called treasure. As if that was ever going to happen.

17

MARTIN rang the doorbell at two o'clock sharp the next day, but there was no sign of David, only a hubbub of conversation and laughter from the back of the house. He rang again, leaning on the bell for a long time. Finally a young woman in a flouncy off-the-shoulder dress threw open the door, a glass of wine in her hand.

'Well, hellooo,' she crooned. 'Either Linda's latest PA really is twelve, or you've come to see David.'

She tottered back up the hall in her high heels, and Martin followed. The courtyard at the back of the house was crammed with people, all waving wine glasses and talking at once. Martin stood on tiptoe and waved to David, who was pressed up against the side fence. Looming over him was Roger Mason, the local historian and antique dealer, a portly man in shapeless corduroys, a grubby shirt and a big red bow tie. Mason was talking animatedly, waving his arms around at great peril to other guests. David had a plate in his hand, and was shovelling food into his mouth as fast as he could. He noticed Martin, but gave a minuscule shake of the head and turned his gaze back to Roger.

David's mother materialised.

'Hello, Martin! How nice to see you! Grab yourself something to eat.'

'Oh, that'd be good, thanks ... But actually, I kind of need Dave. There's this maths assignment I have to hand in tomorrow.'

'Well, take some food with you. And maybe you can both come back afterwards.'

On the way out, nicely laden with containers of food, Martin said to David, 'You didn't seem all that keen to get away.'

'Tell you outside.'

Kitty and Andrea, who had been hovering discreetly a few doors up the street, joined them. As they walked towards the park, munching barbecued chicken legs, David explained. 'Roger Mason was telling me about the coal mine. Did you know there used to be a coal mine here?'

'What, right here?'

'Yes. The entrance and the above-ground stuff were right next to Tarcoola until they closed the mine, then they built the factory there.'

'They closed the mine!' said Kitty. 'That's exactly what she said. Miss Gordon's father used to work there. The Pit, she called it. But I didn't know it was in Balmain. I always thought coal mines were ... I don't know, somewhere far away.'

'So the shafts and all the tunnels . . .' began Martin.

'You got it,' said David.

'That day we went exploring,' said Martin. 'David's Leap.

Do you remember? There were – I saw something like railway lines way down below us. That's what they have in mines.'

'And when my candle went whoosh and burnt my hair,' said Andrea, 'that was methane, wasn't it? There's methane in coal mines.'

'You're right!' David looked at her in surprise.

'Well, what do you think I'm doing in Science?' she challenged. 'I haven't exactly got an iPod in my ear.'

David made an 'I surrender' sign. 'Methane's one of the reasons they closed it,' he said. 'People would get poisoned, or they'd light those lanterns they had and, you know – KABOOM! Roger told me.'

'They had canaries, didn't they?' said Martin. 'They kept canaries in those mines, and if the canaries died, you know, from the gas, because they're so little . . .'

'That's where she hid it!' Kitty ran ahead and stopped in front of the others, blocking their way.

'You have to take me seriously now, you have to. It all fits. Her father worked in the mine. She said he knew where everything was. She said all the canaries died. She said that. Andrea, you know her. She's not mad.'

Martin groaned quietly. The others looked at each other.

'She said, "The wolf boy can't go there. It's safe." Now I know what she meant.'

Still nobody spoke.

'Well, if you're not going to go into that mine, I am!'

'Wait, Kitty!' David grabbed her arm. 'I believe you. But

you can't just go charging in there. We need a map of the mine, at least. He said there's information on the internet. Maybe there's a map?'

Kitty stamped her feet in frustration. 'It'll take too long!'

'Sounds like there's only one way in,' said David. 'Roger says if the development goes ahead they'll build over the last access to it, and the mine will be sealed forever. He says that means losing our history, and they shouldn't be allowed to do it.'

Now Kitty had tears in her eyes.

'Listen, Kitty,' said David gently, 'let's just do a search. We'll find out as much as we can, then go in and have a proper look, see if your old lady's got something hidden down there. Okay?'

'Okay.'

'Now, we can't go back to my place, or we'll get sprung. So let's go to yours. We can eat this kugelhopf when we get there.'

'Right.' Kitty brightened.

The O'Briens' house was tidy and quiet, except for the low humming of the dishwasher and the rhythmic thwack, thwack of the printer. They went into the study, where there were open books and piles of printouts.

'One of your parents has been busy,' remarked David, sitting down at the screen.

'It's Mum,' said Martin. 'She's doing this course. Just leave all her stuff and switch to my login.'

On Martin's page, the New Mail icon was flashing. At the top of the list was a message titled 'Ha ha ha look what my brother snapped'.

Andrea leaned in for a closer look. 'Who's Sam?'

Too late, Martin snatched at the mouse. Andrea had it in her hand and had clicked the message before he had fully taken in the situation.

The message itself was brief: 'Hey lover my brother took this picture with his new iPhone. Nice or what? Catch up soon. Sam.'

The picture, which was right there in the body of the message, in full colour with sharp detail, showed a foolishly smiling Martin being kissed by the lovely Samantha Buckingham.

Martin stood paralysed in the silent room as the others stared at the screen.

'That's Samantha Buckingham,' said Andrea. 'Jeez, Martin!'

'She's all right,' said Martin. 'She asked me out.'

'You can't go out with that snooty, stuck-up bitch!'

'What! Who do you think you are, telling me what to do?' Stung, Martin spoke louder than he intended. His words hung in the air, then there was a flurry of movement and the front door slammed. Andrea was gone.

'Andrea's right, Martin,' said Kitty. 'I think Sam Buckingham's father might be the wolf boy. See, the other day I went to visit Miss Gordon, and . . .'

Martin turned on her.

'I've had enough of you and your fairy tales!' he shouted. 'All this buried treasure and the Big Bad Wolf. Grow up!'

'Come on, Marty,' started David.

'No, that's enough. Enough!' Martin stormed out, ran up the stairs to his room and slammed the door.

He threw himself down on the bed. Who did David think he was anyway, always right about everything? And as for Andrea – there she was at school with those slutty girls, all sniggering at him, skipping Maths with the moronic boys from 7B who were always smoking down by the bike sheds.

He picked up the fantasy novel he had been reading, the fifth in the series, but he couldn't get into it. Resentment seeped through him like acid.

How could a good day turn bad so quickly? Nobody had asked if any of this was his fault. He couldn't really blame Samantha, though. She wasn't to know what an unreasonable lot of friends he had.

His thoughts strayed to the food they had picked up at David's house. Would Kitty think to keep a piece of kugelhopf for him? Probably not, he thought, feeling extra sorry for himself. She and David were probably polishing off the rest of it right now.

18

DAVID walked the streets in a daze. A minute ago he had been having the time of his life, surrounded by friends and full of purpose. Now, suddenly, he was alone, with nowhere to go but home, where his parents' party would still be in full swing. He wished there was a secret entrance into his house, so he could get to his room without being spotted.

KITTY sat in front of the computer, eating kugelhopf and trying to make the internet work. The cake was usually such a treat, with its layers of lighter-than-air pastry shot through with gooey chocolate, but today she ate mechanically, without enjoyment.

Nothing was going right. Whenever she tried to connect to a website she got that horrible error message with a list of pointless suggestions. Marty knew how to fix it. He had a special method of unplugging things and plugging them back in, then turning everything on again in a particular order; but she wasn't game to try that and it was no use asking him. She knew what a slammed door meant.

The extra piece of cake sat on the desk, still in its plastic container. It was meant for Martin, but why should he have it? He'd been down on her all weekend, making it obvious he didn't take her seriously. Losing his temper and shouting at her was just the last straw.

She jabbed again at the internet icon on the computer screen, but the result was the same.

She frowned at the cake. Well, she thought, there's one thing I can do. She picked up the cake and went out in search of Andrea.

ANDREA was pushing her way out through one of the over-grown paths in the Tarcoola garden, twigs in her hair. She had gone in through the factory grounds and spent some time sitting by the fishpond, throwing stones into the water, but it didn't help much. There was still something tight in her chest that wouldn't let go. She thought about going down into the bomb shelter and curling up on one of the narrow beds, far away from people, and staying there for a long time; but at the thought of approaching the house on her own her courage failed.

It wasn't even that she cared so much what Martin did. When they were little, being friends was all about swinging on the monkey bars and jumping out of trees, and that was great. They'd never really had that much to say to each other, and that was okay too. But girls like Samantha made her feel like she was rubbish. Samantha and her friends, with their shiny hair and designer clothes, looked down their sneering noses at her and saw all the things that were wrong with her life. Why did Martin have to say in front of the others that he cared more about Samantha than her? Now her friends made her feel like rubbish too.

The path swung round and ran parallel to the lane, separated by some overgrown shrubbery. She made her way through to the gap in the fence, but when she peeped out into the lane she spotted a small figure trotting purposefully in her direction. It was Kitty, carrying something.

Andrea shrank back into the bushes and inched away from the fence. She couldn't face anyone, or deal with the sort of kindness that Kitty would offer.

She waited, hidden in the shrubbery. A minute or two went by. There was no way Kitty could come through the hole or pass down the lane without Andrea seeing her, but she did not appear.

Andrea edged back to the hole and risked a quick look into the lane. It was empty. She drew back, puzzled. If Kitty had turned around and started walking back she would still be visible. Where could she have gone?

After a few more minutes she climbed out through the hole and turned towards home. There was something odd lying on the ground and she squatted down for a closer look.

It was a small plastic takeaway food container. In it was a generous slice of kugelhopf.

Andrea left the container where it lay and walked home, still wondering. Kitty must have dropped the container, turned back and run away, very fast. Why would she do that?

The shadows were lengthening by the time she got home. Her mother was watching television, a game show.

'There you are, love!' she called. 'Come and help this idiot out. He's got five letters of an eight-letter word and he still can't see what it is.'

Andrea curled up in the threadbare armchair and her mother looked shrewdly at her morose face. 'I was thinking of getting a pizza tonight,' she said. 'What do you reckon?'

'Sure,' said Andrea. 'Where's Celeste?'

'God knows. Off somewhere with the comrades.'

'Who?'

'That new boyfriend of hers is all political. Tells me the revolution is tomorrow – the workers are going to overthrow the bosses. I'd like to be there when they overthrow Dean.' She smiled at Andrea and lit a cigarette.

KITTY had been pretty sure she would find Andrea in the garden. Martin had said it was best to come and go from the lane, so it would make sense to go that way too.

She half-ran, half-walked in the afternoon sunlight, clutching the container, rehearsing what she might say to Andrea. Her legs were still tired and sore from clambering around in the tunnels yesterday, and she was puffing a bit when she turned into the lane, peering at the fence as she hurried along, oblivious of everything else. There had been few people in the streets, and the lane was deserted.

A dog barked in one of the yards backing onto the lane. Kitty took no notice.

Soft footsteps came up rapidly behind her. Suddenly something was flung over her head, scratchy on her face, covering her eyes. A hand clamped over her nose and mouth, and at the same time she was picked up, her arms pinned to her sides. Half-choking, she squirmed and struggled, kicking out. She felt herself being carried at a run, and heard a man's rasping breath.

A car started up and she was bundled in, face-down. Her mouth was free for a moment and she screamed, her voice hoarse.

'Shut up!' Something struck her on the side of the head, then the hand came over her mouth again. Another hand pressed her head down onto the car seat.

They were travelling fast, round one corner, then another and another, changing directions. Dizzy and sick, she tried to count the turns and memorise the route. Her heart was thudding and her hands were cold and clammy.

The journey didn't take long, then she was carried a short distance and dumped roughly on what felt like a concrete floor. Big hands reached under the blanket that was covering her and tied something over her eyes.

'That's too tight,' she whispered, groping at it. Her hand was slapped away, then someone pulled her into a sitting position, her back against something hard and knobbly.

There was a brief silence. The place was cold, and smelled faintly of kerosene. Kitty could sense people near her. All her instinct to escape seemed to have dissipated, and she was trembling.

'Let me go,' she said, unable to stop her voice from quavering.

'You've been a very nosy little girl.' The man's voice was harsh and he spoke right in her ear, his breath on her cheek. She recoiled and jumped up.

'Sit down!' It was another voice. Someone gave her a shove and she stumbled and fell to her knees. 'You don't move until I say you can move.'

Behind the blindfold, Kitty clenched her eyes shut. I won't cry, she told herself. They're not going to see me cry.

'Now,' said the first voice, 'you're gonna tell us what that old bitch has been saying to you.'

'Who?'

Something struck her head again.

'Don't play games with us!' said the first voice. 'What do you think this is?'

Kitty didn't answer. She squeezed her eyes tight.

'You've been talking to her. What's she been telling you?'

'Nothing.'

'Don't give me that bull!'

'Why would I lie? She's just a poor old lady.' Kitty let the tears flow now. 'I take her flowers. She hasn't told me anything.'

Now the man put his hands on both sides of her face and squeezed. 'Why are you kids hanging around that house, then?'

'No reason! Just playing.'

He released her suddenly and shoved her off balance. She heard footsteps, then whispers as the two men conferred. They seemed to be arguing. A door slammed, and her hand crept up to her blindfold.

'Don't even think about it,' growled a voice.

Her senses seemed to sharpen as time passed. She was aware of a man's breathing, not far from where she sat, trembling. Some distance further away, she could faintly hear a voice. From the pauses, she guessed he was talking on a phone. The voice rose and grew shrill, then stopped abruptly.

More footsteps, then she was grabbed by one arm and dragged to her feet. The man walked quickly as she stumbled along beside him, her arm hurting from his grip. She was preparing herself to scream as soon as they got outside, hoping she would recognise the feel of the outside air; but before she knew it she was pushed into the car again, her interrogator beside her with his hand over her mouth, and they were driving.

'We're gonna let you go this time,' a man's voice said, close to her ear. 'But when you see the old lady, you're going to ask her something for us, and you'd better get an answer. You understand what I'm saying?'

Kitty could only make *Mmmm, mmmm* sounds.

'She's got some papers that don't belong to her. You find out where she's put them, and tell us next time.'

The thought of a next time made Kitty feel weak inside.

'That's right, girly,' hissed the man. 'You know what's good for you – and your brother, too. He likes his soccer, doesn't he?'

Kitty started to struggle. She needed to tell him that Martin had nothing to do with this. The man tightened his grip on her.

'I knew a kid, good football player, only he had an accident, broke both his legs. Real sad. Never played again.'

Kitty strained against his hand.

'You just give us what we want next time,' said the man soothingly, 'and everything'll be okay.'

The car stopped.

'And keep your mouth shut. You tell anyone about this, we'll know about it.'

The man reached across Kitty, then she felt herself being pushed out through the open door. She heard the door shut and the engine accelerating. By the time she had ripped off the blindfold it was too late: the car had disappeared.

For a moment she had no idea where she was, then she recognised the street. It wasn't too far from where she lived. But her legs were shaking and the walk home seemed to take forever. It was a shock to reach her own house and to find it looking completely normal, as though nothing had changed in the world.

The front door was wide open, light streaming out and

music playing. Her parents were bringing bags and boxes of garden clippings through from the back yard and placing them on the footpath for the green waste pick-up.

'About time, Kitty!' called her mother. 'It'll be getting dark soon.'

'Yeah, sorry,' she muttered, hurrying upstairs to the bathroom. She washed her face and peered at her reddened eyes. They didn't look too bad.

Martin's door was shut. She tapped lightly, then opened it. Martin was sitting at his desk, drawing.

'I don't want to talk to you,' he said immediately.

'But there's something I have to—'

'I mean it, Kitty. Go away.'

'But I just wanted to see what you . . . what if—'

Martin half-rose in his chair. 'Out, now!'

Kitty withdrew to her own room and sat on her bed, unable to make up her mind what to do. Her hands were still shaking.

She longed to tell her parents. Her father would make those men sorry they had ever come near her. But how would he find them? She hadn't seen their faces, or the car, and she had no idea where they had taken her. What would her parents do?

She pictured them all going to the police station, and the police not even believing her. But the men would be watching, and they would know that she had told. She shuddered.

Her parents would believe her. This was like their worst fears coming true. And of course she would have to tell them the whole story, about the house, and the tunnels, and the treasure. After this she would never be allowed near the house again.

If she had her own phone, like so many of her classmates, she could call someone for advice. The men would never know if she talked to Andrea or David, or even Rosa. Why wouldn't her parents let her and Martin have mobiles?

'Kitty?' her mother called. 'Could you come and set the table, please?'

She went down to the softly lit dining room, her mother's favourite tablecloth folded on the table. There was a glass jug filled with fresh flowers on the sideboard, and the smell of roast chicken wafted through. She could hear her parents laughing in the kitchen while her mother stirred the gravy and her father sliced the meat.

She couldn't tell them.

At dinner, Kitty's father said suddenly, 'There's a sort of protest meeting at the Town Hall tomorrow night, about that development Harold Buckingham's planning.'

'The one where they're going to pull down that lovely old house?' asked his wife.

'Yeah. I think I'll go along, make sure he doesn't get off too lightly.'

'I thought you said your rabble-rousing days were over, Paul?'

'Well . . .' he winked at Kitty. 'Gotta do something when greed rears its ugly head. Harold Buckingham thinks he owns this suburb, and someone has to tell him he doesn't.'

Martin got up abruptly and took his plate into the kitchen.

'Can I come, Dad?' asked Kitty. 'I wouldn't want to miss that.'

'Yeah, why not? I'll show you what a real live villain looks like.'

'Buckingham?' said his wife.

'The same. *By the pricking of my thumbs, something wicked this way comes.*'

They both laughed. In the kitchen, Martin ran water and rattled the plates noisily. Kitty shivered.

19

THE Town Hall was packed for the meeting. David's father had come home unusually early so that he could attend, eating his dinner standing up in the kitchen, a raincoat still flung over one shoulder and his briefcase by his feet. There were more people arriving as David walked up with his parents and Moshe, and no seats left by the time they had squeezed into a middle row. David caught sight of Kitty with her father on the far side of the room. In sign language he tried to enquire where Martin was. Her elaborate answer probably meant that Martin was sulking in his room and not talking to her. Or perhaps it meant that she wanted to talk to him, David. It was hard to tell.

As soon as the traditional acknowledgement of Aboriginal ownership was over, a rowdy group in the front rows jumped up and started waving placards and shouting. Andrea and her sister Celeste were among them.

Annoyingly, most of the placards were turned towards the front, so only the meeting convener and the handful of Council officials on the platform could read them. Fascinated but slightly embarrassed, David tried to get a better look. Among the slogans he could read were 'Leave our park alone',

'No more McMansions' and 'Ban Buckingham Palaces'.

The meeting convener spoke into her microphone: 'The Council does acknowledge your right to express a view, but I have to warn you that anyone interrupting the legitimate speakers will risk being ejected from the meeting.'

There were some boring speakers then, droning on and on about planning laws, zoning and something called non-conforming use. Then the architect for the development got up slowly. He was a small man in a soft grey suit, clutching several rolled-up plans that he occasionally attempted to flatten out on the lectern. The gist of his explanation was that, much as he would like to oblige residents, he needed to use all the space that the site provided, and he needed to demolish Tarcoola to make room for more apartments. He 'could not, *could not*' build fewer apartments.

'There is provision,' he said, 'for the developer to make a cash payment to the Council in compensation for . . . for loss of open space.'

Hands shot up all over the hall. Someone shouted, 'That's a travesty!' The protesters took this opportunity to jump up and wave their banners.

'Order!' shouted the convenor. From the waving hands, she selected Kitty and Martin's father, who stood up and looked around the hall.

'For a start,' he said. 'That cash payment is for situations where there's no open space to work with, as you well know. In this case . . .'

The convenor interrupted him. 'Could you please state your name and address, for the record?'

'Sorry. Paul O'Brien, 39 Donald Street.'

'And did you have a question, Mr O'Brien?'

'Yeah, I do. When you say you can't build fewer apartments, do you mean you've got a target to make a certain amount of money? A profit you're aiming at?'

The architect spread his hands. 'Well, that's not really for me to . . .'

Paul O'Brien bored on. 'Can we hear from the developer? I see he's here at the meeting. Harold, suppose you tell us where you stand?'

All eyes turned to the back of the hall, where a balding man in a suit stood not far from the exit. He gave a little laugh.

'Hey, I'm just the client here. I'm not across any of the numbers. Rudy here and his people are the ones with the big picture. You might want to give him some questions on notice or something. He could put some more FAQs up on the website.'

People were shouting and jeering, but the architect began talking rapidly, saying something incomprehensible about infill housing and the jagged edge. David craned his neck to see the man who must be Harold Buckingham, now heading for the exit. He had been joined by two more men in suits. One was tall and lean with red hair, while the other was short and thick-set, his dark head shaven and tattoos showing on the back of his neck. As soon as most people had turned back to the architect, all three slipped out.

When David turned back towards the front he saw the protesters were milling around, but Andrea remained rooted to the spot, gazing towards the exit, her face white with shock.

David looked in Kitty's direction. She was straining to catch his attention, pointing to the exit, nodding vigorously and attempting to express something in incomprehensible sign language. It seemed to involve pointy ears.

'Order!' said the convenor again. The meeting resumed. Then David realised his grandfather was speaking.

'More than seventy years ago,' he was saying, 'a man came into our community. He came here to escape terrible oppression. He came here hoping to make a better life for himself. And in doing so, he hoped to enrich the life of this community.

'My parents came from a different part of Europe, but they came here for the same reason as Josef Woolf: to escape from the Nazis. They didn't move in the same social circles as Josef. In fact, my father Isaac was a stonemason, and he worked on the restoration of that beautiful garden, which had been laid out in the eighteen-nineties. He used to talk with Josef in Yiddish, and Josef told my father he had made plans to ensure the house and garden would never fall into disrepair again. Ultimately, he intended to make a gift of the estate to our community for everyone to enjoy.'

There was applause and some people stamped their feet. The convenor leaned forward, an expression of long-suffering patience on her face.

'Moshe, it pains me to interrupt one of your stories, but are you asking a question or moving a motion?'

David's grandfather held up a hand.

'One minute. I'm getting there. This is the point of the story: officially, Josef Woolf died intestate, but the residents' action group is not convinced that he didn't make a will. Even today, the ownership of this property is quite unclear. Mr Buckingham is said to have inherited the property but, although he would not like this widely known, the original title deeds are missing. That's at least two vital documents that should have been among Josef Woolf's effects when he died. Now, whether they were lost, destroyed or merely hidden—'

A growing hubbub forced the convenor to shout 'Order!' again.

'. . . we are of the belief that there should be a concentrated effort to find them. The title deed is necessary to clear up the question of ownership, and the will should tell us once and for all what Josef Woolf's intentions were regarding this property. Therefore . . . therefore!' He raised his voice above more excited chatter. David exchanged glances with Kitty.

'Therefore I move that the Council further delay consideration of this application . . .'

Now the architect was scattering his plans in agitation. The rest of the meeting was a blur of unimportant detail as far as

David was concerned. His mind was racing and he just wanted to get outside and confer with Kitty and Andrea.

After the meeting, while people were shaking Moshe's hand or clapping him on the back, Kitty and Andrea both reached David's side at the same time.

'Those men with Buckingham,' said Andrea. 'They're the ones who tried to grab me!'

'Tried to grab you?' said Kitty. 'When?'

'On Friday, after school. I had to hide out at David's house.'

Kitty grabbed Andrea and started to shake her. 'Why didn't you tell me?'

'Hey, Kitty! Chill! What's wrong?'

Looking round nervously, Kitty told them about her ordeal of the night before. The others were horrified.

'You're sure those men with Buckingham are the ones you saw?' David asked Andrea.

'Positive. What did your men sound like, Kitty?'

'I don't know. Scary.'

'Did they have New Zealand accents?'

'I don't know, I can't really tell. But I'm sure now that Buckingham's the wolf boy.'

'How come?' asked Andrea.

'I went to see Miss Gordon one day and she was upset, because the wolf boy had been there. And the nurse told me she'd just had a visit from Mr Buckingham, and he pays for her room. If Mr Buckingham is supposed to have inherited the property he must be descended from Mrs Woolf. The

Woolf boy, see? It all adds up. He's got her there so he can keep asking her about the treasure. She said, "He's at me and at me, but I won't tell."'

David glanced over her shoulder, then looked around desperately for an escape route. Bearing down through the crowd was the unkempt figure of Roger Mason.

'Dear boy!' he carolled. 'I've got something that might interest you.' He shoved a piece of paper at David, then was carried off in a wave of people.

'What are we going to do?' said Andrea. 'We can't risk you going to the house again, Kitty.'

David was skimming through the tattered pamphlet. It was about the coal mine.

'Look,' he showed the others. 'There's a bit of a map here. The tunnels actually go out under the harbour. Look at this: "Sinking of the first shaft, named the Birthday, started in June 1897".'

'Let me see that!' Kitty grabbed the pamphlet. 'Birthday! The other shaft was called Jubilee. Look, Andrea. Look, it's marked on the map. Birthday is just north of the house. That must be where that locked door in the shaft leads. That's where it is!'

'What makes you so sure?' asked David.

'The first day I met her, the first weird thing she said . . . I asked her about her birthday, and she got all paranoid, and wouldn't tell me. She must have thought I was asking her about the Birthday shaft!'

'I still don't get it,' said Andrea. 'What did she hide, and why?'

'We can't be sure until we find it,' said David. 'But hey, it's got to be these missing documents. Maybe there's something in the will that explains everything. I bet Buckingham wants to find it so he can destroy it.'

'Maybe there's treasure as well,' said Kitty hopefully. 'Can we go tomorrow?'

'Not you,' said David. 'Not after what those men said.'

'David's right,' said Andrea. 'He and I can do it. Hey, if they're watching you it'll keep them off our backs, won't it?'

'There's one more thing, though,' said David. 'We've got to find the key to that door.'

'I'll get it,' said Andrea, her eyes sparkling. 'Miss Gordon will tell me where it is. I'll go and see her tomorrow.'

'But I don't think . . .' Kitty protested.

'Kitty!' Her father was beckoning, and she turned to go.

'We'll get the key tomorrow and do a proper search!' hissed Andrea. 'I'll call you after we've been down, okay?'

David ran to catch up with his own family and fell into step beside Moshe.

'So, where are you going to look for this will?' he asked, fishing.

'No idea.'

'Do you think it might be in the house somewhere?'

'Behind a secret panel in the library?' His grandfather smiled and ruffled his hair. 'That'd be nice.'

'I heard someone say there was a second wife,' David ventured. 'Someone Josef Woolf married while he was living here. Has anyone asked her about the will?'

'That's not exactly it,' said Moshe. 'From what I've heard, he was living with the housekeeper at one time. In those days there would be a sort of pretence of marriage, just to look respectable, and it seems she lived in the house for a while after he died. But eventually his wife came back and kicked her out, and she was never seen again.'

'She'd be over ninety if she was still alive,' chipped in David's mother. 'I doubt if we'll be hearing from her.'

David smiled a little to himself as he trailed after them in the dark.

20

MARTIN was sitting at his desk doodling when Kitty and their father came home. He could hear them all talking in the living room, and he resisted the urge to creep to the top of the stairs and listen in. A few minutes later Kitty peeped around his door.

'Are you talking to me yet?'

'Who said I wasn't talking to you?' said Martin tersely.

'Well, not you, because you haven't been talking to me.'

He threw a rolled-up pair of socks at her, and she edged into the room and sat on the bed.

'Do you want to hear about the meeting?'

'No.'

'Marty, you're not really being friends with Samantha Buckingham, are you?'

'Why shouldn't I?' He could feel the heat coming into his face, and he willed it away.

'You do know that her father is the one who's going to do that development, and pull down Tarcoola?'

'That's never going to happen.'

'It is, Martin, if we don't stop it. And anyway, I have to warn you . . . There're these scary men, and I think they . . . they want to hurt us because we're getting too close.'

'Scary men? You've been watching too much television, Kit.'

'No, it's true, and we're ninety-nine per cent sure they tried to kidnap Andrea the other day. They're Mr Buckingham's goofs, you see, and . . .'

'His what?'

'You know. Men in suits with dark glasses. They know stuff about us.'

'Goons. Get it right, Kitty. And you don't expect me to believe any of this, do you?'

'That's probably why she's chasing after you. Samantha, I mean. Her father's probably making her do it, to spy on us.'

'Shut up, Kitty!' Martin's face was bright red now.

'Well, why else would she . . .'

'Get out!'

Martin resisted the urge to slam the door after Kitty. Her story was ridiculous. Was she making it up to get him interested in that stupid old house again?

He packed up his homework things and mechanically got ready for bed, his thoughts on Samantha. They had met after school that day. 'For coffee', her email had said, which made him nervous. He had only tasted coffee once or twice, and it was horrible, even with lots of sugar. But when he got to the cafe in Rozelle she had already bought and paid for a hot chocolate for herself, so it was easy for him to follow suit. This also allayed his other fear, that he would have to pay for her and that he wouldn't have enough money.

Samantha was great. For a start, she was really interested in soccer. Her mother was English, she explained, and a fanatical Tottenham Hotspurs follower, so she was genuinely enthusiastic and agreed with him that there was nothing hard to understand in the offside rule. Then they got onto games. In her house, she told him, they had a special games room, with every game, electronic and otherwise, that he had ever heard of.

'My dad buys them for Oliver,' she said, 'and he loses interest after about five minutes. So then I get to play whatever I want, whenever I want!'

Martin realised his mouth was hanging open.

'It's a pity, though,' she said. 'None of my girlfriends are into that kind of thing. They just want to swap makeup and stuff. So sometimes I wish I had someone who'd come over and play with me.'

He couldn't quite form the words. So he said, 'I thought you'd be into makeup too, not games.'

'Oh no, I've always wished I was a boy. I'd much rather run around and climb trees and stuff than be all girly.'

He stared at her manicured hands and her perfect hair. It was hard to imagine.

'You don't know how lucky you are,' she said wistfully. 'We've got all these things at home, but we're hardly allowed out, except to go to school. It's all "Don't do this, don't do that. It's too dangerous, there's germs, blah, blah, blah." I bet you and your sister get to run wild, all over Balmain.'

'Well, we don't exactly run wild.'

'But I bet you're allowed to go to parks and places like that without your parents?'

'Well, sure.'

'Well, then, you've got lots of places where you can have fun and do stuff we'd never be allowed to do, right?'

'Yeah. It would be awful if we had to stay at home all the time.'

'Like, you know, that old house and garden near the park?' she persisted. 'I always imagine it's like Sleeping Beauty's castle, because the garden's so overgrown. Or some other place in a fairytale. And me and Oliver, we've always wanted to go and play games in there, and hide and – oh, I don't know – look for secret passages and stuff.'

'There are secret passages!' whispered Martin.

'See!' She was thrilled. 'You get to find out this stuff. Oh, I'd love to see something like that. Are they in the house?'

'Yeah, I guess there's one in the cellar, but the really cool one is in the garden, and it was me who . . .'

He became uncomfortable all of a sudden, aware she was staring intently at him, her hot chocolate forgotten.

'But it's not a secret if I talk about it, right?'

'Right!' She laughed. 'But maybe you'll show me some day? We could go exploring together.'

The idea of Sam spying on him was ridiculous. But thinking about it now, he wondered how they had got onto the subject of the house and the secret passages so easily. Had she been pumping him? And had he given anything away? He fell asleep wondering.

21

KITTY agreed to go to Rosa's house after school. It was better than being around Martin, who was still in his bad mood at breakfast time.

On the way, while Rosa chattered cheerfully, Kitty's eyes were everywhere. Before long she was convinced there was a white car following them. It would drive off for a while, then come back. Was it the one that had been outside the Sunset Home the day she'd seen Mr Buckingham there? Her stomach clenched into a painful knot at the thought.

'Kitty!' Rosa's voice broke into her thoughts.

'Huh?'

'I said, what do you think?'

'Oh . . . sorry.'

At Rosa's she tried to concentrate on her friend's chatter, but she kept wandering over to the window. She could see the street, and a white car parked halfway down. Was it the same one? She hadn't thought to look at the numberplate.

'Kitty, what's wrong with you?' demanded Rosa.

'Sorry,' she said again. 'Can I use your phone?'

With some difficulty she composed an SMS to Andrea: 'How's it going? Will she tell you?'

'You don't have to write proper sentences and stuff!' said Rosa, peering over her shoulder.

'It's done now.' She pressed the Send button.

The answer came back in seconds:

'wont talk 2 me wants u'

'What's this about?' asked Rosa.

'Can I borrow some clothes?' said Kitty. 'I need to go out the back way, and I need you to cover for me. I promise I'll tell you all about it later.'

'You'd better,' grumbled her friend. 'What sort of clothes?'

Five minutes later, wearing Rosa's jeans and an old baseball cap, Kitty emerged from the lane that hooked around and came out into the street thirty metres behind the white car. She walked briskly away, resisting the urge to run, her palms clammy. When she got around the corner and out of sight her legs turned to jelly and she almost collapsed. Then she did run, as fast as she could.

At the Sunset Home there was no one around. Kitty waited a few seconds for her rasping breath to quieten, then she hurried up the stairs to Miss Gordon's room.

Andrea sat on a chair by the door, and the old lady was dozing on the bed. She looked unbearably fragile, her hair spread out on the white pillow, her breathing hardly a sigh. At Kitty's arrival she drifted into wakefulness and held out her arms.

'It's Kitty! I thought you weren't coming back.'

'You shouldn't think that.' She leaned forward and kissed the soft cheek.

'I missed my cup of tea. They don't leave it if I'm asleep.'

'I'll make you one,' Andrea said. She slipped out of the room while Kitty helped Miss Gordon to sit up in bed, fetching an extra pillow that had fallen onto the floor. Andrea came back with tea and held the saucer for the old lady while she sipped.

'Ah, good girl. Just the way I like it.'

Kitty said, 'Andrea's my friend, Miss Gordon. She came here with me, remember?'

'Oh. Are you Tarcoola girls?'

'Sort of,' said Kitty. 'Miss Gordon, we're worried about your present. We think the Woolf boy is trying really hard to find it.'

The old lady started to tremble. Kitty put an arm around her. 'The thing is,' she said, 'we can help. We can put it in a much safer place for you.'

'It's safe there,' whispered Miss Gordon.

'Maybe not for much longer,' said Kitty. 'Even if the Woolf boy doesn't find it, he's going to make it much harder to get into the mine. That's where it is, isn't it?' The old lady nodded. 'It's in Birthday, isn't it?' Another nod.

Kitty took the cup, then held the old lady's trembling hands in her own.

'Miss Gordon, can you tell us exactly where it is?'

'Well, he didn't put it right in the shaft, dear,' said Miss Gordon, her eyes far away. 'They were going to fill that in. He said he'd put it where he kept his lunch pail. No one ever touched another person's lunch pail.'

Kitty spoke very seriously. 'Miss Gordon, would you give us permission to find your special present and put it in a safer place, to make sure the Woolf boy doesn't get it?'

Miss Gordon nodded.

'Are you sure?'

'Yes, Kitty. I'm so tired. I can't keep him off any longer. You look after it now, dear.'

Over her head, Andrea mouthed a big 'Yes!'

Kitty raised the bony hand to her lips and kissed it.

'We need the key,' she said. 'There's a big door that goes into the mine, and it's locked. Do you know where the key is?'

The old lady smiled. 'It's with the naughty little boy. That was Mr Woolf's idea. The little boy always made him laugh. He called him Oskar.' Her expression changed. 'After his little boy that he lost in the war.'

'He had a little boy?' Kitty was startled. Nobody had ever mentioned a child before. All of a sudden the cold-hearted and selfish Mr Woolf seemed different to her. He had lost a child! For a moment she glimpsed the darkness in his soul.

She realised that Andrea was making time-to-go movements.

'Where is this—' Kitty started, but Andrea was nodding vigorously and making a sign with her finger and thumb, indicating that she knew exactly what Miss Gordon meant by the naughty little boy.

They ran down the stairs. Andrea opened the big front door

and peeped out, then she jumped back, colliding with Kitty.

'They're there!' she said.

'But . . . but I left them outside Rosa's!' whispered Kitty. She opened the door a crack and peeped out. The white car was parked in the street outside. The sight of it made her start to shake again.

As they stood in the hall a man came down the stairs, balancing a huge white bundle on one shoulder, and set off down a short passage to the left.

'After him!' hissed Andrea.

The man went out a side door, where a blue van was parked. He tossed the bundle in and was about to close the van's sliding door when a voice called out to him. A couple of nurses from the Home were sitting on a bench in the front garden, smoking. He strolled over to join them, lighting up as he went.

The van hid the girls from the smokers and from the street as they slipped out of the building.

'Come on,' whispered Andrea. 'We'll have to hide behind all this laundry until he closes the door.'

They climbed into the van, crouched down and waited interminable minutes, rolling their eyes at each other and not daring to make a sound. After a last burst of laughter they heard the crunch of gravel as the man strolled back, then a scraping, rolling sound as he shut the door. A few seconds later the engine started and they were moving.

'Andrea,' whispered Kitty. 'It stinks in here. I can't breathe.'

'I know. I reckon some of those old people wet their beds.'

'They do more than wet their beds,' complained Kitty. 'I think I'm going to throw up.'

'Don't you dare.' Andrea was busy sending a text to David: 'got it c u in 15 at little boy with fish'.

'Fifteen minutes? How do you know?' said Kitty. 'Maybe he's going into the city. Maybe the laundry's in Parramatta.'

If they went all the way to Parramatta she couldn't imagine how they would get back. The combination of worry and nausea made it impossible to think properly. She tried holding her nose, but that only made it worse when she had to let go and take a deep breath.

After a few minutes the van stopped, then backed up, parking.

'What are we going to do when he opens the door?' hissed Kitty.

'Run.'

The door slid open and they erupted out of the van. Andrea was halfway down the street by the time Kitty registered which way she was going. The man was too startled to react as Kitty took off, his shout ringing in her ears. She pounded along, knowing she'd never catch Andrea, just trying to keep track of which way to go. Gradually she recognised that the van had stopped at a laundromat in the main street and that Andrea had turned the nearest corner and was heading down towards the park.

By the time she reached the garden Kitty's chest hurt, her

legs hurt and she had a stitch. Andrea was waiting for her.

'Where now?' panted Kitty.

'Shortcut.' Andrea plunged into the bushes, and Kitty struggled after her.

David was waiting by a dried-up pond that Kitty hadn't seen before. In the middle was a statue of a little naked boy, surrounded by goldfish.

'Oh, I get it,' said Kitty. 'Isn't he cute?'

'You shouldn't be here,' said David. 'You'd better go home.'

'I can't,' said Kitty. 'If I go out into the street those men'll see me.'

'They were outside the Sunset Home,' Andrea explained. 'We smuggled ourselves out. It was cool.' Her eyes were shining.

'They've been in the house, too,' said David. 'I went down to the cellar while I was waiting, and they've fixed the bolt on the trapdoor and put a new padlock on it.'

'So,' said Andrea, 'they do know about that entrance, and they can get into the tunnels themselves.'

'What about the marks we made,' asked Kitty anxiously, 'leading to our secret exit?'

'Well, luckily we were using Marty's mysterious medieval map system,' said David. 'I'm betting those guys won't have any idea what his symbols mean.'

'At least Marty did something right,' said Kitty. 'Making us find that other entrance.'

'Yeah. I called him and tried get him to come with us, but he wouldn't even talk about it.'

Andrea was looking around the pond.

'Let's find that key and get going,' she said.

They examined the statue first. It was broken in places, but they could imagine what it would have been like intact. There weren't any obvious hiding places, particularly as the little boy was naked. Nor were there any recesses in the pedestal he stood on.

'Okay,' said Andrea. 'It's got to be the fish.'

The key was in the mouth of one of the fish – or rather, down its throat. It was David who worked it out, by noticing that only every second fish was designed to spout water.

'It wouldn't be in a watery fish,' he explained. 'It'd rust in no time. See, it's sure to be an iron key . . .'

'We get it, we get it!' Kitty and Andrea were running around peering down the throats of the non-watery fish, which were turned slightly away from the pond, and it was Kitty who found the key, wrapped in a piece of heavy, oily cloth. As soon as she held it up the others were off, and with her shorter legs it was all she could do to keep up with them.

They regrouped at the edge of the clearing with the female statue.

'Now,' said Andrea. 'Let's be really quiet when we go to the entrance, and make sure there's no one around.'

'Just a minute,' said Kitty. 'Can I please use your phone, David?'

She dialled her home number. Martin answered.

'Is Mum home yet?'

'No.'

'Good. Marty, you've got to cover for me.'

'Huh? Dave said you weren't with them.'

'Well, I am now, but I'm supposed to be at Rosa's. If I'm late, try to stall Mum and Dad, okay?'

'Yeah, but, you know . . . don't be too late.'

'I know, I know. But your precious Harold Buckingham and his gooks are onto us. This is our last chance, Marty.'

'He's not my Harold Buckingham, Kitty, and they're not . . .'

'Sorry, gotta go now. Bye.'

David had gone ahead, so she slipped the phone into the pocket of her jeans.

They moved the pile of stones aside and climbed down through the entrance behind the statue. Staying close together, they followed Martin's symbols back through the tunnel to the main shaft under the house. The solid locked door opposite them was coated with dust and looked as if it had not been moved for a long time. The key fitted easily, but resisted all attempts to turn it. David tried to jiggle it, but it wouldn't move. He tried pulling it out a bit, then pressing it further in, without success. Finally Andrea, with gestures and raised eyebrows, suggested they retreat to the bomb shelter.

'I thought we might oil it,' she explained when they got there. 'That works with our back-door key. There must be some kind of oil here?'

While Andrea lit candles, Kitty searched around and found

something that she thought might do. She also found some kerosene and an old rag, and set to cleaning the key. Meanwhile, David selected three gas masks and tried them on to satisfy himself that they were working. Andrea giggled nervously at the sight.

'We won't be able to talk with these on,' he remarked. 'So it'll be all sign language. Kitty, keep yours simple, okay?'

'I'm really good at sign language!' She was indignant.

'Yeah, but we're really bad at reading it.'

Holding the gas marks and torches, they went back into the shaft and slipped the prepared key back into the lock. At a nod from David, they all found a grip on the key and twisted together. Slowly it turned, and they heard a dull clunk. The door creaked as it swung open and a foul smell erupted into the shaft. Kitty fell to her knees, gagging, her eyes streaming. Next minute they were all tumbling back into the shelter, and Andrea was slamming the door.

'Oh, that was stupid,' gasped David.

Kitty grabbed a bowl and vomited into it.

'Sorry, sorry!' she choked.

They sat around for a few minutes, their heads on their knees, then Kitty got some water from the barrel and they all had a few sips. There was nowhere to tip out Kitty's vomit, so she put the bowl under the table and covered it with newspaper. The smell seeped through, making her nauseous all over again.

'Standing there with our masks in our hands!' said Andrea

shakily. 'What did we think we were doing?'

'Look,' David said. 'If everyone's all right now, let's get the bloody things on, and if we can get from here to the door without killing ourselves, we go into the mine, okay?'

'Okay,' the others agreed.

They put the masks on, carefully adjusted them and gave each other the thumbs-up signal, then set off back to the door. The masks smelled bad, but nowhere near as bad as the gases around the entrance to the mine. At first Kitty felt panicky, wondering what would happen if the smell made her throw up again into the mask while they were inside. After a while she got used to it and her stomach settled, but she wondered what the chemical in the mask was and whether it would run out, and she didn't like the reduced field of vision. She trudged along between the others, trying not to breathe deeply.

The door led into a tunnel much like the ones they had already explored. It appeared to be a natural fissure that had been enlarged and shored up here and there, with a few steps cut into the steep sections as it went steadily downwards. After a short time, it ended in a narrow cleft. When they squeezed through, they were in a wider, higher tunnel which they all recognised instantly as part of a mine.

David gave another thumbs-up signal, and indicated that they should turn to the left. As they walked close together, guided by his torch, Andrea played the beam of the other torch over the shiny black walls and ceiling, shored up with heavy timber beams. There were no signs of life down here: no insects, no cobwebs, no roots of plants straggling through. It was very hot, and the air seemed to shimmer.

Ahead, the tunnel suddenly widened into a roughly round chamber, about four metres across. A door-sized opening opposite them was blocked with a mixture of rubble and a cement-like substance. Andrea pointed to it and nodded vigorously. That must be the Birthday shaft.

Around the chamber, there were the remains of some wooden structures, bits of machinery littering the floor and some steel shelving built into the walls.

Andrea started looking under things on the floor, but Kitty shook her head firmly. She mimed eating and drinking, and pointed to the shelves, which appeared to be empty. The two girls started to search the walls systematically, looking for any niche or recess. Somewhere safe. Meanwhile, David was searching through the machinery. Kitty knew that was wrong, but the gas mask was making her brain foggy, and she couldn't think up the sign language to tell him.

In one section of wall some natural hollows had been enlarged and used to store small objects, like the pigeonholes the teachers used at school. Most were empty, but a few held bits of rubbish: a screwdriver, a rusty old hammer. Then Kitty found a mug with a broken handle; then a tin plate. She was on the right track!

Right at the back of the next niche she saw something crumpled.

Kitty reached in and felt something greasy and yielding.

She recoiled. Then she reached in and felt it again. It was something hard, wrapped in the same kind of stiff cloth as the key and tied with coarse string. She carefully drew it out and looked around for the others. Sign language was all very well, but they weren't looking in her direction. She called out, making a muffled, echoing sound:

'Aahhhhhheeeeee!!'

Andrea jumped. They both turned, and Kitty held up the package. Handing her his torch, David carefully peeled back part of the cloth, revealing the corner of a wooden box. They exchanged a jubilant high-five, then Kitty clutched the package to her chest as they turned and headed for the way out.

22

MARTIN was trying to read a poem for English, but he couldn't seem to make it mean anything. He kept reading the first verse over and over again. The words were simple, but somehow the poem didn't make any sense:

> *A narrow fellow in the grass*
> *Occasionally rides;*
> *You may have met him – did you not,*
> *His notice sudden is.*

'A narrow fellow in the grass'? What was that?

He looked at the poem, but the lines blurred. He didn't like the thought of Kitty in those tunnels without him. David had said just he and Andrea were going. Why had they changed their minds? Had something happened?

He didn't have Rosa's mobile number, and he couldn't call her house if she was covering up. It wasn't fair of Kitty. First she made up that ridiculous story about threatening men, now she was getting him and possibly Rosa into trouble.

The house was quiet, but their parents would be home in

an hour or maybe even less. He went downstairs and tried to ring David, but there was no service. They must be underground already. What had David said? There was something down there, just as Kitty had suspected, and he and Andrea were going after it because Kitty . . . because Kitty . . . what had he said? Martin hadn't been listening properly.

It was probably all a load of rubbish anyway.

The phone rang again. He raced to pick it up.

'Marty? Is that you?'

'Samantha?'

'You know, it'd be soooo much easier if you gave me your mobile number. It was really, really hard to get your landline. I tried White Pages but it seems to be a silent number. I suppose it's because of those nuisance calls, my mum says . . .'

'Samantha, what do you want? You could've sent me an email.'

'I guess so. I just . . . I sort of wanted to know if you were at home.'

'You're not thinking of coming round, are you?' Alarming thoughts flashed through his brain.

'No! No. Anyway, I'm not allowed out, unless it's . . . No. Just wanted to make sure you were okay.'

'Why wouldn't I be?'

'No reason. Only my dad . . . He was kind of mad about something today, something to do with that house of his. I heard him talking on the phone to those men who work for him. He was saying something about some kids, and after that stuff you told me about the house and the tunnels, I was worried that you might have gone there.'

'After that stuff I told you?'

'Yeah. I think it might be a good idea if you don't go there for a while.'

'What do you mean, stuff I told you?'

'Look, Martin, I'm sorry, I'm really sorry. My dad gets those things out of me. You don't know what he's like.'

'Samantha! What are you talking about! What did you tell your dad?'

'What you told me.'

'But I didn't tell you anything! Did I?'

'Well – just a little bit. About the secret entrances. One in the cellar and one in the garden.'

He sat down heavily on the stairs.

'So you went out with me because your dad told you to? To find out what we knew?'

'No! I mean, he told me to, but I did it because I like you!'

Martin was on the verge of slamming the phone down, then he finally registered something she had said.

'What men?'

BACK in the shaft under the house, David re-locked the door into the mine and they thankfully removed the gas masks. Kitty opened her mouth to speak, but Andrea put her finger to her lips and pointed upwards towards the house.

'Let's get out of here,' whispered David. 'All I want right now is to breathe fresh air. Then we can whoop and holler or whatever we're going to do, and we can have a good look at this thing.' The others grinned and nodded.

MARTIN got to the house and found the glass doors still unlocked. He crept in and down the cellar stairs, all his senses alert. The trapdoor was exposed and bolted down with a shiny new padlock. He stared at it, the hairs on the back of his neck prickling.

THEY made their way back to the entrance in the garden, Kitty still clutching their prize, and David went up the ladder and peeped out cautiously.

'It looks clear,' he whispered to Andrea.

She climbed out after him. There was a sudden rustle and she felt herself grabbed from behind. Before she could scream, a hand was clamped over her mouth. At the edge of her vision she could see David in the grip of a tall, red-haired man, kicking and struggling furiously.

'Wow!' said Kitty, emerging behind her. 'This is the best day . . .'

Her voice trailed away and she turned to run. The short, stocky man who was holding Andrea took a firm grip on her upper arm.

'Yis, sure uz,' he agreed in his strong New Zealand accent.

'You're sure that's all of them?' said the taller red-haired man.

'Yeah, the other boy went straight home from school and stayed there.'

Kitty started trembling so hard she nearly dropped the package. Andrea squirmed and kicked out, trying to reach the red-haired man's ankles.

The man evaded her easily, and held out his hand for the package. Kitty clutched it closer to her chest.

'You think you're so tough,' she said, 'Spying on kids, and . . . and going round being Mr Buckingham's ghouls!'

Andrea gave a nervous giggle. The man leaned forward casually and slapped Kitty hard on the side of the head.

Andrea screamed. Kitty staggered, fell to her knees and dropped the package. She didn't make a sound, but Andrea could see tears running down her cheeks. In the brief confusion David broke away from his captor, dived in and grabbed the package. He looked around wildly then started to run, but the red-haired man caught him before he had gone more than a couple of paces.

He twisted David's arm roughly up behind his back. Andrea could see that it hurt, and that David was struggling to keep his face expressionless.

'Try that again and I'll kill you.' The man's voice was cold and detached.

With the tall man still holding David's arm at an uncomfortable angle behind his back and the shorter man following, dragging both girls by their arms, they set off in an untidy procession.

At the edge of the rose garden they had to go into single file to pass through a break in the stone wall. Pushing David ahead of him, the red-haired man suddenly stumbled and, with a curse, fell forward. There was a flurry of movement and a yell of pain from the other man, then he too was down.

Andrea grabbed Kitty by the arm. 'Run, run!' she yelled.

The taller man was already up and grappling with Martin, who was wielding a long piece of wood and trying to hit him again with it. The man shouted, 'Don't let them go!' Meanwhile, David had broken away and run back into the rose garden.

The short man grabbed Andrea. Seeing this, his partner let go of Martin and tried to get back into the rose garden, but the short man, confused, had dropped Andrea's arm and now had Martin in his sights. The two men collided in the gap, cursing and shoving at each other. With seconds of freedom and nowhere else to go, David ran back behind the statue and dropped into the tunnel.

The tall man grabbed Kitty and Andrea roughly by the arms and dragged them over to his partner, who was holding Martin. Martin was scratched, dirty and defiant, kicking out whenever he could.

'You're bloody useless,' growled the tall man to his companion. 'You caught the wrong one. Take care of the lot of them.' He pulled a gun out from under his jacket. 'You'll need this. Lock them up in the house, then get the fuel out of the car. I'll grab the other one.'

With that, he disappeared behind the statue.

The short man waved the gun at the two girls.

'All right, get over here and get in line.'

'You wouldn't use that,' said Andrea.

'I'll try this first.' He held up his other hand threateningly. She shuffled into line, scowling furiously. They moved off towards the house, the man bringing up the rear just behind Kitty. Andrea kept hearing the other man's words. 'Lock them up in the house, then get the fuel.' What did he mean? What sort of fuel?

'You'd better let us go,' said Martin. 'I told our parents exactly where I was going. They'll be here any minute.'

'That's an old one,' sniggered the man.

'It's true,' said Andrea. 'These two are on a really strict curfew. Their parents always come looking for them.'

'Pull the other one.'

Andrea and Martin exchanged glances, and Martin gave a wry little shrug. Kitty suddenly stopped dead.

'Watch out!'

23

DAVID ran blindly down the tunnel, blundering into walls as he groped in his pocket for the torch. Flicking it on, he took stock of his situation without slowing down. Where to go? With the trapdoor now padlocked he wouldn't be able to get into the house. Could he try losing himself in the network of tunnels that led to David's Leap? No, his pursuer would just sit tight and wait for him to come out again. Or follow him in and . . .

He still had the big iron key. Would there be time to get to the bomb shelter, grab a mask, unlock the door and get into the mine? Probably not, and anyway, he didn't know any other way out from there either. *Not enough data*, he kept thinking as he pounded along. *Need more input.* As he rounded a bend he saw a flash of reflected light on the wall ahead. Someone was already on his heels.

He had reached a junction that he knew well. The path to the right would take him to the house and the mine. The one to the left would take him to the caves in the cliff and the Doughnut. With no time for hesitation, he turned left.

'IT'S a snake!' said Kitty. 'Nobody move!'

Now the short man was really exasperated.

'Git going!' he yelled, his accent thickening in his exasperation. 'You kuds thunk you can take the puss out of me just cause I'm a Kiwi!' And he pushed Kitty roughly, making her stumble forward into Andrea. 'Even I know there aren't any snakes in the . . .'

The snake struck low and hard, biting the man just above the ankle. He screamed, dropped the gun and started hopping around on one foot.

Andrea quickly kicked the gun into the undergrowth out of sight. The snake flexed and was gone. Martin stared after it, transfixed.

'A narrow fellow in the grass occasionally rides,' he said dreamily.

DAVID could hear sounds behind him when he reached the end of the tunnel. Water was at his feet. He realised that he had no idea whether it was high tide or low tide, no idea how long the tunnel was, how far he had to go, how long it might take. His brain, which automatically calculated everything in sight, had nothing to work with. *Insufficient data. No more inputs.* But someone was coming up rapidly behind him, he could be certain of that. His whole life had come down to this moment, and no matter that his mouth was suddenly dry and his stomach was clenched with fear, there was only one thing he could do, and he had to do it now.

KITTY was pulling at the man's arm. 'Stop that, stop that!' she shouted. 'You're supposed to keep still. The poison works faster if you jump around!'

'Come on,' cried Andrea. 'Leave him!'

'Hey, we've got to help him,' objected Kitty. 'He's been bitten by a snake! He'll die!'

The man screamed louder.

'Kitty, a minute ago he was going to lock us up and—'

'I know, I know, but we've got to help him.'

'We've got to help David!' said Martin.

'I know . . . Let's take him to Cec's house. The back gate's just through there. We can just yell out to Cec, and leave him in the back yard.'

'You take him,' said Andrea. 'I've gotta go.'

She fled up the path, through the garden and into the park. She reached the cliffs and clambered down, her feet slipping on loose rocks, almost falling in her haste. The tide was halfway out, water lapping all around the Doughnut and half-filling it. She squatted on a nearby rock and waited, her heart pounding.

DAVID tucked the package securely into the front of his shirt and turned off his torch. He took a couple of deep breaths for practice, then filled his lungs.

He swam from memory: a few strokes above the surface, a deep breath, then under. Swimming down and down in the black water, away from the air, was terrifying. A light flickered onto greenish rock as his pursuer reached the water's edge. When it was gone the darkness was profound, but then he felt something scraping his knees and realised he had reached the lowest point and the tunnel was starting to rise. His heart soared, but the strain was starting to tell on his lungs, and he still had no idea how far it was.

His chest was hurting. An eerie light shimmered around him but the tunnel seemed endless, and a little voice whispered that he might have taken a wrong turn somewhere. If he reached a dead end he would not be able to turn back.

With the last of his strength he kicked his legs as hard as he could.

ANDREA squatted on her rock. It was taking too long. She knew David would not have gone any other way. She refused to think about the tall man catching him down there. She stared at the Doughnut without blinking.

Suddenly water erupted from the rock. A head shot up, then disappeared. A couple of seconds later David emerged, shakily pulling himself up, gasping, streaming water. Andrea was with him in a couple of strides, and by the time she had helped him out she was almost as wet as he was. They clambered up the cliff and lay on the grass at the top for a moment, panting.

David took great, shuddering breaths, still unable to speak. He patted the bulge at his chest and nodded, to show her that the box was safe, and she jumped up and danced a little victory dance before sitting down again.

They watched the Doughnut for a few minutes, but nobody emerged. The man would not have known that you could get out this way – he was probably searching the tunnel for other exits, wondering where David had gone.

David looked back at Andrea. She was wet, dirty, smeared with coal dust from the tunnels, her hair was sticking out in all directions and she was smiling radiantly.

When he got his breath back, he said, 'Will you go out with me?'

24

KITTY and Martin took one arm each and half-dragged the man as he stumbled through the shrubbery. They guided him through the hole in the fence to the lane behind Cec's house.

The back gate was unlocked. As they pushed through, a cacophony of barking started up.

'Get it off me!' screamed the afflicted man.

'Don't be silly,' said Kitty. 'She's just being friendly.'

Sweetheart blundered around, impeding their progress and nipping at their feet, and Cec came to the back door to see what was going on.

'Cec!' called Kitty. 'Can you please call an ambulance? This man's been bitten by a snake.'

'I knew it!' Cec's face lit up. 'Didn't I always say there was snakes? I knew it!'

Win's face appeared at the door, and she and Cec drew the frightened man inside.

'Right,' said Kitty. 'Now let's grab some axes or whatever we can find in Cec's shed, and go after that . . . that . . .'

Martin looked at her with astonishment. Her fists were clenched and her round face was flushed with determination.

The thought of her taking on the tall man was almost comical, but something warned him not to laugh.

An unfamiliar ringtone started to play. Kitty looked around, puzzled. 'Surely Cec and Win haven't got a . . .'

Martin said, 'Kitty, it's you.'

'But I . . .' She fumbled at her clothes. 'Of course, I've still got David's phone.' She pulled it out of her pocket. It was Andrea.

'Kitty? I'm with David. He swam the Doughnut!'

'Wow! Is he okay?'

'Yeah, look, we're going to his place so he can dry off. Get over there as quickly as you can.'

'Right!' She slid the phone shut. 'Sorry, Cec,' she called. 'We have to go. Emergency at home.' She grabbed Martin's arm.

'Thanks for looking after our friend here,' Martin called as they ran back towards the back gate. 'Can you get his name and address? We want to send him a Get Well card.'

On the way, Kitty asked a few awkward questions, but before long she was puffing too much to speak. Martin simplified his story, saying that he had started to worry after her phone call, and had finally decided to go looking for them.

'When I saw the padlock on the trapdoor, I thought there might be trouble,' he said, 'so I found that bit of wood in the cellar and went down to the other entrance near the statue to wait for you. I was only just in time.'

Andrea answered the door at David's house.

'David's just getting some dry clothes on,' she said.

As they crowded into the kitchen, David's grandfather came in through the back door.

'Hello!' he said. 'Martin and Kitty, you look like children who've been up to something.'

Andrea shrank back behind Martin. The old man smiled at her.

'And an ally in the cause!'

'Huh?'

'Did I not see you at the Town Hall last night, exercising your citizen's right of dissent?'

'Oh, umm – yeah, I suppose so.'

'I'm Moshe.' He held out a hand.

'Oh, hi. I'm Andrea.' They shook hands. 'Actually, we've got something here . . . David wants to show you himself.' She put her hand on the package.

'Really? Intriguing. I think this calls for tea,' said the old man, switching on the kettle.

By the time Moshe had handed out herbal tea and home-made biscuits, and Andrea had unwrapped the box and set it in the middle of the table, David had joined them and his mother had come home.

'What's all this?' she said.

'I promise you'll get all the details later,' said David. 'But this box was more or less hidden in Tarcoola. Harold Buckingham has been trying to find it, and we got there first.'

'You have to be joking!'

'No joke, Mother. Shall we open it?'

They all leaned in.

'Tell you what,' said David kindly. 'You do the honours, Kitty.'

Trembling, she fumbled with the unusual catch. Then there was a faint click and the box sprang open.

Nestled in a bed of deep blue velvet was a glittering necklace. It was set with colourless stones which caught the light. The centrepiece was a small, richly coloured red stone.

Nobody spoke for a moment. David's mother stroked the red stone. 'It's pretty,' she said at last.

'So it is treasure, Kitty,' said Martin flatly.

'Listen,' Andrea addressed Moshe directly. 'We went through a lot to get this. Some men were going to kill us for it.'

Moshe stepped out the back door and called out, 'Roger? Are you at home? Would you care to come and look at something for us?'

A minute later Roger Mason was at the door, perspiring curiosity. He peered at the necklace through a jeweller's eyeglass.

'Very nice, very nice. Worth a bit. Josef Woolf, you say? Yes, he would have brought it from Prague, certainly. Could have been his mother's. Not real diamonds, of course, but nicely made. That's a garnet, not a ruby. Hard to put a value on it. Could be in the thousands, I suppose. Rather lovely . . . Hmmm.'

His attention wandered.

'Personally, what I find more interesting is the box.' He

picked it up and ran his fat fingers over it. 'Beautiful piece of work, this. See how the design is continuous as you move over the different surfaces? But what's *really* intriguing about these boxes . . .' His hands were busy. 'There's nearly always a secret . . .' – suddenly there was a sharp click – '. . . drawer!' The bottom section of the box popped out, revealing a compartment stuffed with papers.

The phone rang.

'It's your mother, Martin,' said David's mother. 'She's looking for you and Kitty.'

'Oh no!' Martin grabbed the phone. 'Sorry, Mum. Yeah, I ran into Kitty, so we were coming home together. Yeah, sorry, David fell in the water and we just came home with him while he . . . No, he's fine, he's fine . . . No, we didn't . . . No, it's all right. We'll be home really soon.' He hung up. 'Parents! Oh, sorry.'

Moshe was going through the papers.

'For a start,' he said, 'Here are the title deeds to a house – that will be Tarcoola. Yes, there's the name.'

David's mother pounced on the documents.

'A will,' she said. 'What we want now is a will.'

Moshe kept looking. 'There are a few things here,' he said. 'Two or three letters, certificates . . . Sorry to be slow, but this stuff is in several languages, some of which I don't know. But I can't see anything that looks like a will.'

He looked worried. 'There's definitely not a will in English or German here. There's some stuff in Czech, which he would have spoken, but nothing that looks remotely like a will to me. I can't be sure until we get it all translated, though.'

'This is not good news,' said Roger Mason. 'The title deeds and no will. This is just what Harold Buckingham needs.'

'Can't you just hide them again?' pleaded Kitty.

'Darling, you do know I'm a lawyer?' said David's mother gently. 'There's this inconvenient thing called professional ethics. He owns the house, so technically this stuff belongs to him and we are obliged to hand it over.'

'That sucks!' said Martin.

'Hey, I'm just the messenger. And by the way, I'm not asking yet how you kids got hold of this stuff, because there might be a teeny matter of trespass.'

'But Mum,' protested David, 'You're not going to just call Harold Buckingham, and tell him to come and get his prize?'

'No, of course not. I'll make it as hard as I can. Papa, how long will it take you to go through all that other stuff? Maybe there's something in there that can help us.'

'No problem, Linda. If you can hold off until the end of the week, I'm sure I can get to the bottom of this. There has to be a good reason why Josef Woolf put these documents in a box and hid them.'

'That's right!' said Kitty. 'It's going to be all right!'

'Ah, the optimism of the young,' sighed David's mother.

25

'DAVID'S parents have invited us for lunch,' said Kitty's mother. 'The whole family. Won't that be nice? I don't know where Linda finds the time to cook, with that job of hers, and Alex works horrendous hours.'

'They all cook,' said Kitty. 'And David's grandad makes great cakes. I can't wait. I really, really can't wait.'

Kitty rang David. 'Does this mean Moshe has sorted out all that stuff?'

'Looks like it. He won't tell me anything yet. He's been having a ball – on the computer and the phone all day and all night, faxes flying everywhere. And I don't know what he's come up with, but it can't be all bad. I've never seen him so excited.'

ANDREA said to her mother, 'We're going to lunch at David's on Saturday. You're invited too.'

'Oh, sorry, love. I'll probably have to work a double shift.'

'Mum, they're really friendly people. They're not, you know, snobby. It'd be so good if you could come.'

'Well, I'll try and get away. You go, love, but tell them not to wait – tell them I'll get there if I can.'

HELPING his mother in the kitchen, David said, 'I still think we should have gone to the cops about those men.'

'I know the cops,' said his mother. 'You wouldn't have got a hearing.'

'That tall one threatened to kill me,' persisted David. 'And he said "Lock them up in the house and get the fuel." What do you think he meant by fuel? I think they were going to burn the house down, maybe with us inside it.'

'Did you hear him say that, about the fuel?'

'Well, not me personally, but . . .'

'David, men like that, stupid men, will say anything to scare kids. It's not a crime. It's only a crime if they actually do something.'

'He pulled a gun!'

'Evidence?'

'Well . . . Marty went back to look for it, but it disappeared.'

'Soooo . . .'

'He hit Kitty. Knocked her down.'

'Yes, and she didn't have any bruises. I know, I'm talking like a lawyer again. See, it's only your word, the four of you, against theirs. You were trespassing on private property, and as far as I know those guys were employed by Buckingham as some sort of security. They don't seem to be around any more, by the way. He's got a couple of Korean guys now. I think he likes the new image.'

'That man is an . . .'

'Don't say it, David. Your father is allowed to use bad language because he has a stressful occupation. That doesn't apply to you.'

'Okay, Your Honour.'

ANDREA and the O'Brien family arrived together. The kitchen table was laden with food, and there were extra chairs arranged in the living room. Roger Mason had been invited too, and he was eying the table, clearly eager to get started.

'Martin and Kitty tell me you've got some sort of announcement to make,' said Paul O'Brien, shaking Moshe's hand. 'What exactly have they been up to?'

'Suffice to say they stumbled on some old documents,' Moshe replied smoothly. David caught Kitty's eye behind her mother's back. She nodded at Moshe and grinned approvingly.

'I've been sorting them out and having them translated,' Moshe went on, 'and once we've got ourselves something to eat, I'm going to tell you all a little story.'

'What sort of documents?' asked Kitty's mother.

'They're related to Tarcoola – to the development,' said David's mother. 'That's what Papa's going to tell us about. We want to know whether it's good news or bad news for Harold Buckingham.'

'Aha! Bad news, I hope,' said Paul.

'Buckingham knows we've got them,' said Moshe. 'I've had a threatening letter from a solicitor, saying I'd better hand them over. He probably thought Linda and I put you kids up to the whole thing.'

David's father came downstairs, holding a laptop.

'Put that away!' said his wife.

'Oh! Sorry – forgot I had it.' He disappeared again, re-appearing empty-handed a moment later.

'No phone?' She patted him down. 'Okay, you're good.'

They all started circulating the table, piling plates high with food. As they settled on chairs and couches and started eating, there was a ring at the door.

David's father came back, chatting animatedly to Andrea's mother, who was pink in the face and silent. David's mother stepped forward.

'Chris! Great to see you. Grab a plate, you've got some catching up to do. Now, red or white wine?'

When they were all settled Moshe refilled his glass, spread out the box and its contents on the coffee table, and began.

'This story starts in 1932, when Josef Freudenthal married a lovely young woman called Naomi Weinsheimer. Well, let's surmise she was lovely. You'll allow me some poetic licence here.'

He held up a marriage certificate.

'Josef was a Czech national, some sort of industrialist with interests in various German cities as well as Prague. The happy couple set up house in Berlin, and their lives were complete with the arrival of a son, Oskar, in 1935. Here is the birth certificate.

'But the 1930s, as it turned out, was not a good time for a young family in Europe. Not if you were Jewish, anyway, like the Freudenthals. Things came to a head on the night of the ninth of November, nineteenth thirty-eight. Hatred, stirred up by Hitler for his own purposes, boiled to the surface. People rampaged through the streets of German cities, attacking Jews and wrecking their shops and businesses. They call it *Kristallnacht* because of all the broken glass. On that night many Jews were killed and many more were taken away, nobody quite knew where.

'Josef and Naomi were in Berlin, at the epicentre, and we can only imagine their terror. Afterwards, they seem to have made up their minds that Naomi and little Oskar would be safer in Czechoslovakia, so Josef sent them to Prague.'

He held up a handwritten note.

'This,' he said with pleasure, 'is in Yiddish. I had to enlist the help of my old friend Arnold in translating it. Yiddish was spoken in Jewish families right through Eastern Europe before the war. My parents spoke it when I was young, but I'm pretty rusty now. The letter says, more or less, "Dearest Josef, I miss you, I hope you are being careful, I pray that this madness will end soon and we can come home, etcetera."

'Well, as we know, the madness didn't end, and things got very bad very quickly for Jews in Germany and Czechoslovakia. So Josef Freudenthal hatched a plan. He moved his money out of Germany, probably into Switzerland, and got himself a new, false identity – Josef Woolf. Now we find Josef Woolf marrying an American woman called Myrtle Carlyon.' He held up another marriage certificate.

'An American woman?' cut in Andrea. 'But is she . . .'

'The dreaded Mrs Woolf, yes.'

'The Mrs Woolf who came here after the war?'

'Yes.'

'But does that mean she wasn't really . . .'

'Let's finish the story first, then we'll discuss the implications, hmm?' Moshe shuffled the papers, looking for the next bit of evidence.

'Now, Naomi knew about this sham marriage . . .'

'Wait a minute,' said Kitty. 'Did he marry this American woman or not?'

'He married her,' said Moshe patiently, 'but it wasn't legal because he was still married to Naomi. It was what's called bigamy. I'm afraid Josef Freudenthal – or Josef Woolf if you like – was a bigamist.'

'Oh, poor Myrtle,' said Kitty.

'No, not poor Myrtle at all. She knew quite well what she was doing. Josef was a rich man, and he would have paid her to do this. See here, we have another letter from Naomi, in which she says . . . hmmm . . . "Tell Myrtle I'm grateful."'

'Why would they do that?' asked Kitty's mother.

'I would assume it was because Myrtle was American,' said

Moshe. 'She could get him out of Europe, to America. Once he got there, he probably planned to go back to his original identity and arrange to bring out Naomi and the boy. Of course, he had no idea that that would have been impossible. Impossible.'

He sighed heavily and gazed at the floor, lost in thought for a while. The others waited politely. At last he resumed.

'However, it seems Myrtle got cold feet in September 1939, when war was declared. So she deserted him, leaving this note: "Dear Joe, Getting too hot round here for little old me. See you in Berlin or New York after the war, depending who wins. Look after all that loot, honey. I've got your IOU for my share. So long, Myrtle."'

'Charming,' said Andrea's mother.

'What's an IOU?' asked Andrea.

'Literally, "I owe you",' explained David's mother. 'The plan must have involved him paying Myrtle more money when they all got to America.'

'So what happened next?' asked Kitty, bouncing with impatience.

'Well, there's a big leap here, because we find Josef in Australia, having managed to bring his money and get himself established here. No doubt his idea was to set himself up somewhere safe and send for his real wife and child.

'However, in October 1939 the Nazis began to deport Jews from Czechoslovakia to Poland, transporting them in locked passenger trains. Those who survived the journey were put into Polish ghettos. It seems Naomi and Oskar went to the Warsaw ghetto.

'Conditions in the ghettos were bad, very bad, and thousands of people died of starvation and random killings. In early 1941, Josef received this letter from a friend, smuggled out of Warsaw. The letter's in Czech, so I had to have it translated. With it is a death certificate in Polish. I had a Polish friend look at it, just to make sure.'

His sombre expression was enough to tell the rest. Kitty and Andrea were both crying. Kitty's mother bowed her head and covered her eyes.

David's father brought in a tray of coffee, and Moshe paused to pour himself a cup. When he sat down again the white cat jumped onto his lap and curled up, purring.

'So Naomi died in the Warsaw Ghetto, as did many thousands. Josef never had a chance of getting his family out. Not a chance. I doubt if he ever understood that.'

David's mother Linda got up and went into the kitchen, kissing the top of Moshe's head as she went past.

'After the shock of receiving that letter,' continued Moshe, 'I suppose Josef just threw himself into work. He built up his business, became an important man. And Clarissa . . . I had no idea that Clarissa Gordon was alive, girls, until you told me what you had found out. From what I can gather, she came to Tarcoola originally as the housekeeper. It's a classic story, isn't it? She was young and beautiful, and her world couldn't have been further away from the one he had escaped. I suppose it was her innocence that appealed to him. He doesn't seem to have told her anything about his past. Whatever . . . In January 1942, he married her.' He put a marriage certificate on top of the pile.

Linda started bringing plates of cake and biscuits into the room.

'Here, let me help you,' said Andrea's mother, jumping up.

'Do you know something?' said Moshe. 'I was at their wedding. My parents were invited because my father had worked on the garden.' He smiled at the two girls. 'See that photograph on the wall, with me as a baby? I didn't realise until now what the occasion was, but it's written on the back.'

It was one of those pictures that you never notice because it had always been there, among the other black-and-white family photos. David looked now in astonishment. The slender, bearded young man, clearly Moshe's father, and the dark-haired woman beside him were both focused on the baby in her arms. Behind them he could see a stone wall, just like the one that enclosed the rose garden.

'So Clarissa's marriage wasn't bigamy?' Kitty was saying.

'Certainly not. Naomi was dead, and he was never legally married to Myrtle, so his marriage to Clarissa was quite legitimate. In fact, what we have here is the proof that Josef Woolf, or should I say Josef Freudenthal, was legally married to Clarissa Gordon. As he didn't leave a will, she is his heir, and as she is still alive, she is the owner of all his property, and has been all this time.'

'The mistress of Tarcoola,' said Kitty.

'Quite.'

'But still,' said Linda, handing round plates, 'wouldn't Buckingham be his descendant? That would give him a claim on the estate. Certainly under German law . . .'

'I'm ahead of you there, my dear.' Her father beamed at her. 'Harold Buckingham is not Josef Woolf's descendant. The internet being a wonderful thing, I was able to discover that Myrtle Carlyon married one Walter Buckingham in Idaho in 1941. Harold Buckingham is their grandson. If Myrtle has no claim on Josef Woolf's estate, then Harold doesn't either.'

'We've got him! Papa, you're a genius. And you kids!' To David's intense embarrassment, Linda danced around, exchanging high-fives with everyone.

'And Oskar?' asked Kitty in a small voice. 'What happened to Oskar?'

'I'm sorry, Kitty. One little boy, in the ghetto . . .'

'Does it say anything more about him in any of the letters?'

'There is only one veiled reference. It says something like "Oskar has been taken."'

'Is that good?'

'No, I can't imagine that's good. I don't think Josef's friend could bring himself to give more details. You don't want me to tell you what they did with small children, now, do you?'

Kitty, Martin and Andrea were wide-eyed, but they all nodded. David shifted uncomfortably. He had heard all this before.

'Well, they rounded them up from time to time and took them away, in trucks or trains. Away from their parents. They took small children, old people, the weak, the sick – anyone who was not useful. They were never seen again. I don't want to say any more than that.'

Kitty's mother hugged her tight.

'But anyway,' said Paul O'Brien, 'all this proves that Clarissa Gordon is the surviving Mrs Woolf, and she really owns Tarcoola?'

'Absolutely,' said Moshe, as the other adults nodded and murmured assent.

'I can sort of understand why Josef couldn't bring himself to tell her the story and left her these papers instead,' said Kitty's mother, 'but why didn't he make sure she understood how important they were, and tell her she must show them to someone after he died?'

'Well, he probably never imagined that Myrtle would ever show up and make trouble. But then Clarissa had a stroke of bad luck.'

He reached over to the sideboard and produced a printout, a facsimile of a newspaper article.

'I went through the newspapers at the State Library with, I must say, infinite patience. I found this small article from 1946. The tone is rather unpleasant so I'll just summarise. Apparently Clarissa was kind enough to put on little garden parties for American servicemen stationed here after they entered the war. One of them happened to be Myrtle's cousin.

He eventually made his way home to some desolate mid-west town, described the experience in detail and told the story of the mysterious Mr Woolf and his suicide. So word reached Myrtle's ears.

'Now I think that, being a bit of a gold-digger and being in possession of her own copy of the sham marriage certificate, Myrtle decided to descend on Australia and claim to be the real Mrs Woolf. It worked like a dream. It's a great pity Josef hadn't told Clarissa that the papers in the box would help her in such a circumstance.'

'Poor Miss Gordon,' said Kitty. 'Mrs Woolf took everything she had. She didn't want her to take the box too, so all she could think to do was to keep it hidden.'

Moshe sighed heavily. 'Josef knew there were bad times coming. But even he never imagined how bad it was going to be. They must have all thought the war would finish, and everyone would go home, and everything would just go back to the way it was before.'

'Come on, Papa,' said his daughter, putting an arm around him. 'We've done something good here today.'

'We certainly have!' He beamed around the room. 'Let's you and I get all this paperwork processed, then we'll give Buckingham the good news. Then Kitty, you can give Clarissa her treasure back.'

Kitty nodded happily.

'I have put the word out about Oskar,' Moshe went on gently. 'I still have quite a network of friends – my parents' friends really – all over the world, and there are organisations that trace people from the ghettos and the camps. Sooner or later we'll find out what happened to him.'

'What are you going to do about the solicitor's letter? From Harold Buckingham?' asked Kitty's mother.

'Oh, Linda's drafting the sweetest reply, informing them that the documents don't belong to him. She'll include relevant photocopies. Wouldn't you love to see Buckingham's face?'

Cleaning up afterwards, David said to his grandfather, 'Those men really were going to kill us.'

'For what it's worth,' said Moshe, 'Josef Woolf would have believed you. He understood that there's evil in the world.'

26

MARTIN picked up the phone in the hall. It was Samantha.

'I don't suppose I should be calling you,' she said meekly.

'Well . . . you know . . .'

'Only, that day we talked . . . later on that day my dad got really, really mad, and he's been really, really mad pretty much ever since. So I wondered if maybe something happened.'

'Why don't you ask him?'

'You're kidding, right?'

There was a silence.

'Well—'

'I—'

'No, you go first.'

'Since you ask,' Martin said stiffly, 'it was good that you called me that day. Whatever those men were going to—'

'Martin, I don't want to know any details, okay? Just that everything turned out all right.'

'Oh. Yeah, everything turned out fine for us. And thanks for warning me.'

'I'm glad I did.'

'So your dad's upset?'

'Spewing.' She gave a little giggle. 'He fired those men. He says New Zealanders are useless. He's got new security guys now, and they don't speak English. He just yells louder, and wonders why they still don't understand what he's saying.'

There was another silence. Then she spoke in a low voice.

'I don't suppose you'll ever want to speak to me again.'

'Well, you know – after that . . .'

'I understand, I really do. I just . . . I just wish I knew before all this . . . I really like you, you know? I wish we could have just met, and had coffee . . .'

'That was good,' he admitted. 'I liked that café.'

'Did you really?'

Martin took the plunge. 'I couldn't do that dance thing, but we could go to the café again, if you're up for it.'

'Sure!'

'Only this time I'll call you, okay?'

'Sure, Marty. Any time.'

CLUTCHING the box, Kitty bounded upstairs, tapped lightly on the door and slipped into the room.

'Hello! I've brought you something. Oh!'

Miss Gordon was sitting in her chair by the window, her soft white hair haloed with light. Her face lit up with a radiant smile.

'Kitty! Look who's here. '

A man was in the room. She hadn't noticed him at first because he was standing by the door, arranging some flowers in a vase on a small cupboard. He was a bit older than Moshe, bright-eyed, alert and well-dressed. He stepped forward and held out a hand.

'Sorry to startle you.' He had a deep, pleasant voice and an American accent. 'I'm Clarissa's stepson, Oskar Freudenthal. I believe I have a lot to thank you for.'

'HIS mother smuggled him out of the ghetto in the early days,' Kitty explained to the others. They were sitting in the grass at the tip of the park, enjoying a sea breeze at the end of a sweltering day.

'Remember that letter that said "Oskar has been taken?" That's what it meant, but they couldn't say it outright in case the wrong people saw it. A Polish family took him in and pretended he was theirs. All they knew was his real name and that his parents were trying to get to America. After the war, when he was old enough, he migrated there himself. He spent his whole life searching, but he couldn't find them. Remember Moshe said there were organisations that trace people? Oskar was in touch with all of them, but he was looking for Freudenthals in America. He'd never even heard the name Woolf. Then Moshe's message went up on some bulletin board, and he saw it!'

'So how does Miss Gordon feel?' asked Andrea. She and

David were leaning against each other, back to back.

'She's come alive. She's got a family now. It turns out Oskar comes to Australia quite often. His daughter lives in Sydney, and there are grandchildren. They're all going to visit her.'

'What's going to happen to the house?' asked Martin.

'Oskar said they'll fix it up eventually, starting with the garden. He's really interested in finding out what Mr Woolf wanted done with it.'

'Can we meet him?' asked Andrea.

'Yes, he wants us to show him the garden, and the little boy of course, and everything else. He's suggested we have a picnic there. I thought on the grass, in front of the lady? He's going to bring Miss Gordon! She can't walk that far, but they have wheelchairs at the home, so he'll borrow one of those. I think we'd better invite your grandfather, David.'

'We wouldn't be able to keep him away.'

'Miss Gordon's going to get dressed up, and she'll be wearing her special necklace. She was so happy to see it again. Mr Woolf gave it to her on their wedding day, and she didn't even know there was anything else in the box.'

'Well, we'll all get dressed up too,' said Andrea. 'This will be a party to celebrate Miss Gordon's new life, okay?'

'Great,' said David. 'We'll bring the food.'

'Am I invited?' asked Martin sheepishly.

'Hey, bring your girlfriend!' said David. Both girls raised their eyebrows. 'She is a direct descendant of the wicked Myrtle,' he reminded them. 'She can do a sort of apology.'

'No way!' cried Andrea, throwing grass at him. His protests were lost in a flurry of arms and legs, screams of laughter and flying grass as the sky turned from violet to pale green and lights flicked on, reaching across the darkening water.